POISON AT PEMBERTON HALL

THE FIRST MYSTERY FOR VITA CAREW

FRAN SMITH

CHAPTER 1

*C*ambridge 1903.

The woman was in a hurry. Pausing at a corner to study a piece of paper, she turned into a side street before reaching a shadowy doorway. There was mud on the cobbles and a thin rain made them shine under the flickering gas lamps.

She knocked, stepping into the entrance to shelter from the rain and glancing up and down the street as she waited.

A broad, dour-faced woman servant, with sleeves rolled back over large forearms, opened the door and led her wordlessly down a gloomy passage into the room at the end. A raised chair stood at the centre. Trays of instruments were laid out in rows on cloth covered tables.

The man neither stood nor turned to look at her but continued stirring something in a glass vial, holding it to the light. He wore a stained white jacket.

'You understand my terms?'

'Yes.'

The visitor reached into her handbag and took several coins from a purse. She held them out, but he gestured with a tilt of the head that she should lay them on a shelf near the door.

'Sit in the chair,' he said.

Shuddering, the woman made no move. 'It must not be pressed or tapped, I beg you. It is so terribly painful.' She held her cheek with a gloved hand.

'It must be lanced and the rest of the tooth removed. There is a risk of poisoning the blood otherwise.'

She hesitated, still.

The dentist sighed, and continued his stirring. 'If it is not treated, it will hurt you more. You have tried the medicine the other dentist gave you?'

'For almost two weeks. It brought no relief. My whole face is affected. I can barely speak.'

It was true. She laboured the words from her mouth between clenched teeth.

The dentist looked over at her for the first time, as if making an assessment. He held out the vial of medicine he had prepared. 'Take this now. It is unusually strong. Only my customary pharmacist will make it up. It exceeds the dosage that is usually permitted.'

The woman clutched her handbag to her chest. 'Will this take away the pain?'

'It will dull the pain while I extract the remaining parts of the tooth.'

She took the vial and held it briefly to her nose. 'And once the tooth is gone?'

'That depends on what I find. This medicine will help. You can take some with you and use it as needed.'

'I must not be drowsy. I have responsibilities. I care for children.'

'Sit in the chair and allow me to examine the tooth.'

Grimacing, the woman swallowed the contents of the

glass vial, removed her bonnet and moved toward the chair. 'You will not tap it?'

'I will do what I need to do.'

The dentist stood, calling out of the door, 'Mrs Griffiths! I need you to hold.'

The neighbours were used to the terrible cries that followed.

CHAPTER 2

The city of Cambridge boasted several long-established pharmacies, their interiors shining with polished brass, their walls lined with drawers labelled in lavishly curlicued copperplate writing: *Tincture of Benzoin, Camphor, Copper Sulphate.* In these establishments customers sat in comfortable chairs whilst the pharmacist and his assistants hurried to fetch, crush, blend, and package the many medicines and appliances on offer. Ledgers recorded every transaction; repeat prescriptions were accurately made up; doctors' instructions carefully followed. Money was hardly mentioned. It was taken by a cashier at a desk in the corner, as if it were an afterthought.

But this particular chemist had no friendly clerk at a desk near the door. Nor were there helpers in white coats climbing ladders to pull exotic herbs and medicaments from high drawers. It did have two large bottles of blue water in the window, but they were dusty, and the curtain behind them had been eaten by moths. The pharmacist, a large man with a boxer's flattened nose and hair oiled into a centre parting, looked more as if he would wrestle customers than serve them

4

politely, but his shop still did steady business. There were no chairs. Nobody cared to dally in the dim interior. Their visits were generally as short as they could make them.

Vita found this place after a recommendation. She needed chemicals in order to carry out the experiments suggested in her Chemistry textbook, but many of the smarter pharmacists showed themselves oddly unwilling to sell them to her. It had never occurred to Vita that anyone might object to a young woman's scholarly purchase of, say, hydrochloric acid or formaldehyde - what business was it of theirs if she carried out experiments in her bedroom? - but the gentlemanly pharmacists looked uncomfortable when she asked for them, and one even asked her to return with a letter of permission.

Aunt Louisa tolerated Vita's experiments and her studies in general, although she occasionally objected to loud explosions or pungent odours, but Vita had no wish to test matters to the limit by bothering her with requests for letters. When Mr Gadd's shop was recommended as a cheap and unquestioning source of chemicals favoured by many students, she went along the next day for some prussic acid and *sal volatile*. The shop, though poorly lit and dusty, had several shelves displaying test tubes, vials and a whole range of glass and rubber experimental equipment, which immediately caught Vita's eye. She was inspecting them when the door opened and another customer stepped in.

The other customer, a thin woman in a brown coat, entered briskly. Pulling her purse from her handbag, she walked straight to the counter and laid her coins in front of the owner without speaking. Equally silent, he glanced at the money, bent slightly to a shelf at knee height behind the counter and produced a stoppered blue bottle which looked small in his broad-knuckled fist. He set it on the counter between them.

'I'll take two bottles this time, please,' the customer said.

The pharmacist was slow to react, but a shadow darkened his expression. He nodded towards the small pile of coins between them.

'That pays for one bottle,' he told her.

Neither looked up. A cart clattered by outside, iron wheel rims grating the cobbles.

'Perhaps you will allow me the second on credit?' she suggested.

The pharmacist drummed heavy fingers briefly on the wooden surface. 'No credit. My customers sometimes forget to pay their debts.'

His hand fell back onto the small bottle and he began to remove it.

'No! I will take that one, if that is all you will allow.'

She tried once again, 'I shall not be able to come next week. They are entertaining at the big house.'

'Which big house is that?'

She seemed unsettled by this sudden interest, hesitating before answering, 'Pemberton Hall'.

'Pemberton Hall? I know a rhyme about Pemberton Hall,' Gadd said. '*Rule at Pemberton, warm and well fed; Serve at Pemberton, early dead.*' He grinned at his customer's discomfort. I have business with one of the servants there. Mr Billings. You know him?'

'Billings? Yes, of course, he is valet to his Lordship,' she said. There was a slight suggestion of distaste in her tone.

'Good customer of mine, is Mr Billings,' said the pharmacist. 'He was here only yesterday.' Gadd leaned over the counter towards her, speaking confidentially, 'You can take the second bottle, Miss, if you promise to send the balance of the money with Mr Billings. He comes every Thursday.'

He placed a second bottle beside the first and slid both

towards her with one hand, shovelling her coins into the till drawer with the other. By the time he looked up both bottles were gone and the door was already closing.

Vita had observed this odd conversation from a corner. The pharmacist had clearly forgotten she was there and registered surprise, and possibly resentment, when he saw her, but was happy enough to sell her a glass retort and the chemicals she wanted. The price was lower than she had expected. No information was requested. No questions were asked. Vita stepped back out into the chilly afternoon with the cheerful feeling of having overcome at least one small obstacle to her scientific studies, even if the details of Gadd's shop lingered uncomfortably in her memory.

CHAPTER 3

'*N*ow Vita, I thought we agreed, no textbooks at the breakfast table.'

The breakfast room at 144 Eden Street was filled with soft winter sunshine. It lit the marmalade and made the silver teapot shine. Vita's aunt Louisa, in her working day outfit of frilled white blouse and dark skirt, poured tea and handed a cup to her niece, adding, 'How is your German, Dear. Didn't you have a Swiss governess at one time?'

The question caught Vita by surprise. 'Yes: Fraulein Weber, but my German is rusty and limited, I'm afraid.' She closed her book, *Studies in Fossil Botany*, and looked over at her aunt.

Louisa flourished the thickly-embossed invitation she had just pulled from its envelope. 'We are invited to Pemberton Hall. A dinner and gala concert. Felicity Pemberton is a dear friend. Her son, Alexander, is my godson. He was a musical scholar here in Cambridge and visited often. A very talented and agreeable young man. He will be performing with Karlotta Von Diepentahl. Have you heard the name? She has performed all over Europe. It should be quite spectacular.' She glanced back at the letter accompanying the invitation. 'Many of the guests will be German. Do you own a formal gown?'

'I have worn my white dress to parties occasionally,' Vita said, but she sounded doubtful.

'You have no evening gown?'

'I never had need of one. There were no parties to go to.'

'Nonsense! Is that what my brother told you? There were several rather grand events in the season when we were growing up in Devon. I have fond memories of dancing until dawn at the Hunt Ball at Waveney House in particular.'

Aunt Louisa looked into the distance with a happy expression. 'Some of the young gentlemen were fine dancers in those days...but that is long ago and beside the point. At eighteen every young woman should own at least one presentable evening gown – one that will serve, with a few adaptations, in every eventuality. Otherwise one must borrow an outfit – which is rarely satisfactory – or even *refuse* the grander kind of invitation, and where will that lead?'

'To a quiet life without tiresome social occasions?' Vita suggested mildly, buttering her toast.

The older lady frowned; she wasn't to be thwarted. 'I shall take you to Miss Pushkin. She is my own dressmaker and very reliable.'

'Oh, but Aunt, I...'

'We'll call there at eleven. And your spectacles, Vita. They are lopsided.'

Aunt Louisa left, heading for her studio.

Vita removed her spectacles and held them up to see where they were bent. The marmalade continued to glow golden in the sunlight.

'*Oh dear*,' she said to the empty room.

It was her first winter in Cambridge. She missed her father and the familiar routine of his Devon parish. An extravagant society occasion with Germans to speak to, and a new gown. The thought of it made her want to hide under the table.

CHAPTER 4

*M*iss Pushkin's place of business was a colourful basement shimmering with rich fabric and beautiful dresses displayed on rows of headless wooden mannequins. The view from the sunken window was of railings, passing boots, and the hems of coats as they swept by at eye level. Vita studied them wistfully, looking up from the soft velvet sofa provided for clients. 'You see, I was hoping to start a programme of reading. I am so very far behind,' she explained to her aunt.

Louisa, perfectly at home in the little basement she knew so well, was browsing bolts of fabric on a broad cutting table across the room, feeling the quality and pulling lengths out to match colours with a painter's eye.

'Pemberton has a wonderfully well-stocked library, you will be perfectly free to use that, Dear. I've known Alexander since he was born. He first met Karlotta at my house. We simply must attend. Besides, they would be so grateful if you could help translate for the German guests. Really, it is a cry from the heart from my oldest friend. Her circumstances are difficult. It would be cruel to refuse.'

Miss Pushkin entered from her sewing room, brisk and elegant in grey silk.

'Miss Pushkin, my niece, Vita, needs an evening dress suitable for a gala occasion. It will be her first.'

Unsmiling, the dressmaker turned her professional gaze to Vita. 'Stand, please,' she said.

Vita stood.

There then followed a long pause while both ladies looked the girl up and down, assessing dressmaking possibilities. They circled her silently. Heifers must feel this way at a cattle market, Vita thought, but did her best not to waver.

'The lighter blue silk, I think,' Miss Pushkin finally declared.

'Perfect,' Aunt Louisa agreed. She and the dressmaker began to delve into the pattern books on the table, turning the pages this way and that, their heads together. Necklines and trim were discussed, buttons were chosen, fittings agreed.

Vita was consulted, but only briefly. Mostly she just sat and envied the passers-by whose boots she could see striding the pavement outside.

CHAPTER 5

*O*n the train her aunt settled herself into her seat. Trunks and hatboxes had been stowed by the porter. Gentlemen waiting on Cambridge station pressed their hats to their heads with gloved hands in the bitter wind. Trees along the line swayed and tossed against a gloomy grey sky.

'Now, Vita, every guest should arrive at least a little prepared.'

Vita had, naturally, brought a textbook with her but she set it unopened on the seat beside her.

'Felicity McMartin - we grew up as neighbours in Devon - married Richard Pemberton almost twenty years ago. Dickie was a younger brother - his older brother Roland was to inherit the title and Pemberton Hall, but Roland died in India quite suddenly, so against expectations, Dickie inherited.'

They watched the gentle hills south of Cambridge roll by the window for a moment.

'Felicity and Dickie began their married life in a perfectly ordinary house. Dickie is a military man - a long tradition in the family. Alexander was born there. But once Dickie inherited the title there was no question of staying, they had to move to Pemberton Hall. I won't bother to describe the place, you will see it for yourself. It was once extremely grand, but when they took possession it had fallen into a state of sorry disrepair. The expense of maintaining a great house and its staff is immense, as you can imagine. They have had to sell a great deal of land, furniture and silverware to cover debts and expenses.'

Her aunt paused as they came into one of the small stations on the branch line and two ladies carrying large baskets clambered aboard further down the platform.

'Felicity had a small inheritance of her own. That, and the fact that Dickie became a horse breeder of some reputation, kept them afloat. But then there was his accident.'

'Tickets please, Ladies.' A uniformed ticket inspector appeared, smiling, and punched their tickets with the flourish of a man enjoying his work.

'It was two years ago now - he was thrown from his horse and severely damaged his back.'

'How dreadful,' Vita said.

'It was. He was bedridden for many months and still suffers from a partial paralysis. Poor Dickie, he is a coun-tryman at heart. Loved the outdoors, always rode and spent his days among horses or on the land. Now all he can do is sit in a chair. It has been terribly difficult for everyone, but for Felicity in particular. Once the charitable visits to the sick man were all completed, very few people continued to call. Dickie locked himself away.'

Vita was familiar with the isolation of a home where an invalid must be the focus of all attention.

Her aunt brightened a little. 'I have visited at least twice a year since, and I am happy to say that little by little Dickie has resumed his bloodstock interests. He has some excellent brood mares, I'm told, and high hopes of one of their recent foals. Work to restore the house continues. It is never-ending. In such a place there is always a leaking roof or rotting timber somewhere, and every inspection finds something worse hidden underneath.'

'Some people think Pemberton is prone to bad luck and accidents. We were once at dinner when a chandelier crashed to the floor in the room next door. The sound was so dramatic that we thought the whole wing had fallen down, but all we found when we dared to look was an empty room entirely coated in broken crystal and a table-sized hole in the ceiling. It was a miracle no one was killed.'

Louisa sighed and smiled at her niece, 'So, Vita, if ever you had fanciful ideas about the grandeur of living in a stately country house, a few days at Pemberton Hall will probably cure you of them. It can be a gloomy old place, but everyone agrees on one thing: the food is excellent. They have rather a famous French chef. Before Dickie's accident Monsieur Picard's reputation alone used to bring eager guests from far and wide. Royalty included! The Hall was famous for its spectacular dinners. They have hardly entertained at all recently, so perhaps this event marks a sort of re-entry into society for them. Let us hope so.'

By now they were slowing and their station, Pemberton Mount Ferrers, was in sight.

'Felicity and the children will welcome you, but Dickie can be brusque. He is in constant pain and tires easily. On social occasions he comes and goes as he pleases. He may appear at dinner, or his place may stand empty, one can never tell. The unwritten rule is to carry on without comment. You will like the children. Mary-Ann loves company, and William is a serious little boy. Last time I saw him his main interest was trains. Wear your bedsocks and an extra vest in bed, and if there are no spare blankets, ask for some – the Hall is notoriously cold. And thank you for coming. I can tell you nothing about the German guests except that they do not seem to speak any English - so if you are the main translator, you are likely to be kept busy.' She looked out of the window. 'And here we are. They are sending the cart with a footman, so we needn't worry about our bags.'

The train pulled into the station, and through the steam of the engine, they saw a tall, uniformed man step forward.

'Mrs Brocklehurst, welcome back!' he said, smiling in greeting and stepping forward to hold a large umbrella over the ladies' heads. 'And this must be Miss Carew.'

'Good morning, Tom,' said Louisa. 'My niece's trunk is near mine and there are two blue hatboxes.'

'This way Ladies,' Tom said. Leading them to a waiting pony and trap, he helped them onto the seat and pulled the heavy cover over their knees before turning back for their bags. Curtains of rain were now falling from low black clouds. The horses splashed arcs of mud as they approached Pemberton. The downpour drenched the branches of the ancient chestnut trees along the drive, and a sharp wind shook the sculpted hedges of the formal garden.

Louisa pulled a paper from her handbag and handed it to her niece. 'Before I forget, Vita, here is something I have devised to keep you entertained,' she said.

They left the avenue of trees and drew towards the great house.

Vita was puzzled and read the paper curiously.

'It is a sort of quest or treasure hunt?'

'It is a list of a few of the paintings in the hall. You are to find them and be prepared to discuss their merits. I thought you would like something to keep your mind active and to practice your powers of analysis. I promised your father that I would add to your education - this will sharpen your knowledge of the History of Art.'

Her aunt was looking pleased with herself. 'I thought you might need the occasional respite from translating. It will give you an excuse to explore the Hall and something to occupy your mind.'

Vita felt her mind was perfectly well occupied already with trying to conquer the basics of Physics and Chemistry, but she liked the idea of a reason to venture about the great house on her own. 'Thank you, Aunt,' she said. She had time only to read the first item: *The Admiral*, before the carriage arrived outside the grand stone staircase sweeping up to the porticoed entrance of Pemberton Hall.

AS THE GUESTS arrived that morning, a tour of inspection was under way in the bustling basement kitchens of Pemberton Hall. Monsieur Picard, the chef; Mr Swain, the butler; and Mrs Dobbs, head cook; were making their morning rounds. All three were senior members of the household with strong views, but here in the kitchen nobody crossed Emile Picard, a distinguished veteran. He had run kitchens far grander than Pemberton Hall's, but these days he chose a quieter life. Older now, his moods could be unpredictable, but his food was reliably magnificent.

Any tension over the demands being placed on the kitchen by a gala dinner with many guests showed only in a general briskness, and Cook's quick steps as she led the two men from one room to another. She was a short, energetic woman, round and rosy cheeked.

'I've had to put the quail in the scullery. They're hanging over the big sinks, Mr Picard. There are too many for the game room. We shall have our work cut out just dressing them all in time. There's pheasant and duck too, but they're in the usual place and most of them's already done. I shall set about the *consommy* soon, did you want your usual *consommy*? It just says *consommy* on my list.'

'*Volailles*, it says *consommé de volailles*, does it not?' said Monsieur Picard.

Both peered at the handwritten menu he held, he squinting at arm's length.

'Ah yes, *volayles*.' Cook, though expert at reading menu French, pronounced the words in an insistently English way. 'Just chicken, or were you wanting turkey or guinea fowl in it as well?'

'Non, non. Chicken only.'

'Right you are. Now, those French oysters. They are in the ice rooms, out by the back door. I shall need a couple of your lads to help with opening the shells, Mr Swain.'

'I can spare Alfred and Tommy, but I'll need them back by five to serve at table.'

'They shall have to work fast, then. Mussels and razor clams, Mr Picard, just a quick scalding?'

'Yes. I shall prepare the sauces myself. They must be presented on the tall ... ' Monsieur had forgotten the word, he waved his hands, ' ... those tall things with many levels ... ?'

'The tiered stands? Yes. We know that, Mr Picard. The venison and lamb you've already seen. The peaches, pineapples and asparagus are in the cold store with the salads. The ice creams are made and in the ice boxes. You will make the jellies, I think?'

'*Oui*. The other pastries also. And the wines, Monsieur Swain?'

'All present and correct,' the butler told him. '*Cham-*

bertin, 1875, Moet et Chandon 1884, Chateau Latour 1875, and his Lordship's choice of port and brandy.'

The three paused and slowed a little. They stood now at one end of a scrubbed wooden table stretching the long length of the great house's vaulted-ceilinged kitchen. On shelves around the walls, copper pans in serried rows glowed in the light of lamps overhead. At one end, the black range with five large ovens and spits large enough to roast a whole pig, seemed still, but the occasional glimpse of a glowing ember and the smell of roasting meat that filled the kitchen showed the fire was alive within and the meal under way.

'Well,' said Swain, 'we seem to be ahead of ourselves.'

'Don't say that, Mr Swain, you'll tempt fate. It's the ice that worries me. What with all this new shellfish from France. Ice isn't easy to come by. It doesn't grow on trees, you know.'

'Can more be found?' Swain asked, fighting the temptation to remind Cook that ice did grow on trees, now and then.

'Not easily. We'd have to send to town for it. There may be enough.'

'And the pastry table is mine from noon, yes?' asked Monsieur Picard.

'We shall clear the far end for your pastry work, as usual, but we shall need to be working at this end. There is still game to be dressed and butchery to be done, as you know.'

'Of course,' said the chef, and placing the menu back in his pocket he turned and walked away.

Cook watched him go before turning back to Swain.

CHAPTER 6

'*H*e upset Cora and Annie again today. Called them clumsy and swore at them in French, poor girls.'

'Do they know French?' asked Swain.

'Well, no, but it sounded rude, whatever he said. He is very hard on my kitchen maids lately, Mr Swain. Can you have a word with him? I do not want them in floods of tears and running off to their rooms. I've quite enough to do without that sort of shenanigans.'

Swain looked up the empty corridor in the direction taken by the chef. 'He is not quite himself, I grant you. There has been a little difficulty,' he said.

'Difficulty?' Mrs Dobbs was suddenly alert. 'What sort of difficulty?'

Both looked up as the figure of Billings, the valet, emerged from a storeroom and moved swiftly to the back stairs leading up to the master's private quarters. Stairs that only he was permitted to use.

'I can't say I like the way that man comes and goes as he pleases, Mr Swain. He's forever in and out of the kitchen making demands. I do not take orders from Mr Johnny-come-lately Billings, nor do my kitchen maids. It's bad enough with that fussy madam Miss Hartley and her finicky likes and dislikes.'

Swain's expression was pained.

'But you were saying something about Monsieur Picard – a difficulty, you said,'

'Yes, a personal matter,' said Swain, clearly weighing up whether to tell the cook more. Mrs Dobbs, reading his expression, looked piercingly up at the butler, who was the taller by at least 18 inches.

Swain took the plunge. 'There is a disagreement between Monsieur Picard and Miss Hartley,' he told her.

'What sort of disagreement?'

'He has confided in me man-to-man. I do not want to betray his confidence, but he permitted me to share the information at my discretion.'

'Yes...?'

'Miss Hartley has made a sudden and unwarranted declaration to Mr Picard. A declaration...of *love*.'

Swain delivered this nugget in the calmest manner, but its effect was to make Mrs Dobbs rock back on her heels and grab for a side table to steady herself.

'She never did!'

'He told me himself. The man was overwrought. She will not leave him alone. She puts notes under his door. She writes him poetry. She hides in corridors and accosts him with gifts. It is quite excessive. He assured me that he has done no more to encourage her than to express an interest in opera. He is fond of it and happened to mention the fact in a brief conversation. Miss Hartley says he has *lit the fire of love* in her heart - those were her words. Monsieur Picard meant no such thing and now he cannot shake her off. He has been direct. He has told her frankly and plainly that he wants no more of it, but she will not desist. He believes it is a kind of madness. An *amour fou*, he called it.'

'Oh my!' said Cook, her hand pressed to her mouth in shock. 'But are you certain Mister Picard has not played on her feelings?'

'I have only his word, but I believe him. He was genuinely distressed. Everything he does to discourage her only makes her more insistent, he says. It has been going on for several months. I tell you this now because I would not wish any short-tempered behaviour on Mr Picard's part to disrupt the kitchen at a time like this. I hope we can keep this matter to ourselves.'

'I shall not tell a soul. I can't bother myself with love at a time like this. What about this shellfish? The first I heard of all this shellfish was Thursday. Whatever gave Mr Picard the idea?'

'I believe someone overheard Miss Karlotta say that oysters were her particular favourite.'

'Someone?'

'Myself, as it happens. I mentioned it to Master Alexander and he insisted they were added to the menu.'

There was a short pause during which Mrs Dobbs glanced sternly upward at the butler. 'I see,' she said, with a grim expression. 'Ah well, French oysters it is. Rather her than me.'

'Perhaps you would prefer a shepherd's pie, such as the one that Annie has cooked for us?' Swain suggested, indicating that they should follow the chef.

'Upon my word I would,' she said, and they moved smartly off in the direction of the servants' dining room.

CHAPTER 7

*V*ita and her aunt were soon beside a fire roaring in the largest fireplace Vita had ever seen.

'I can hardly tell you how relieved we are that you could come,' Lady Felicity said to Vita. 'I do not know how I should have managed. Miss Von Diepentahl has brought her two aunts and their doctor - a very strange little man - with her. With our own family, guests from the university and a few neighbours, we are a party of thirty-two for the concert and dinner. A large party by our recent standards. I expect your aunt told you my husband has been unwell. We haven't entertained on this scale for several years. I'm quite out of the habit. Karlotta and the German doctor speak a little English, but the aunts do not have a single word. Without you it would have been nothing but nodding and pointing - can you imagine! Karlotta always travels with her aunts, apparently, and the doctor was thought a necessity as they were travelling abroad. I suppose English doctors weren't to be trusted. She is making a tour of the country giving performances. Well, I should say she and Alexander together are making a tour. They frequently perform together and have a most enthusiastic following, I'm told, though the world of music is a mystery to me. Alexander, as you know, Louisa, certainly did not inherit any musical ability from my side of the family.'

'How is he enjoying this success?'

'He seems extremely well, his health is good, but he is also very preoccupied. They travel a great deal and there seem to be endless plans and arrangements to be made. Strictly between us, I believe he might be going to propose to Miss Diepentahl. Please say nothing to anyone yet, but it seems a possibility.'

'An engagement!' Louisa said.

'He has said nothing formally as yet. I tell you this in confidence. We knew that he was extremely fond of Lotti, of course,' Lady Pemberton looked into the fire for a moment. 'He can hardly bear her to be out of the room. Follows her like a puppy.'

'Would you welcome such an engagement?' Louisa asked her friend.

There was a moment of hesitation. Vita suddenly felt that the ladies might prefer to speak without her presence.

'I wonder if I might visit the library before luncheon?' she asked. 'If there is a German dictionary, it might help to look at it before I meet the German ladies.'

'What a very thoughtful idea,' said Lady Pemberton and, looking relieved, she pulled a lever beside the mantlepiece to summon the butler.

'Now, Vita, about your room. The German aunts have been very particular about where they will sleep. The housekeeper has had to make several rearrangements. She has put you in the Yellow Bedroom at a little distance from the others. We don't use it very often. The bed is rather extraordinary. I hope you will be comfortable.'

CHAPTER 8

*S*wain, a stately presence in his tailcoated livery, led
Vita down the stairs, across a marble-floored hall
and along a broad passageway before throwing open a pair of
double doors.

The library was huge. Bookshelves ran from floor to
ceiling with ladders on brass rails to reach the highest
shelves. It was also distinctly chilly. The coals in the grand
fireplace were unlit and there was a touch of damp in the air.
At one end a grand piano looked small among several large
desks and sofas.

'I'll send someone to light the fire, Miss,' Swain told her.
'You are embarking on a course of study, I understand? May I
ask which subject is of particular interest? I am familiar with
the shelving arrangement here. Perhaps I can assist.'

Vita, slightly overpowered by the grandeur of the library
and of the butler - most of her reading having been done in
the public lending library or her own bedroom so far - was
touched by Swain's thoughtful offer. 'I am particularly interested in the sciences,' she told him, 'but if there are any

German books, it would be helpful to glance at them too. My German might be a little rusty and I am to translate.'

Swain led Vita to a small alcove on one side. 'The family's collection of volumes on horse breeding is considered very thorough, I believe. There are also one or two books on equine anatomy and medicine. Some quite rare. Biology as a science on its own may only be represented by studies of the flora and fauna of this area. Would they be of any use? As to German books...' Swain moved to another part of the library and indicated a small collection of books in several languages, '...you might find something here.'

'I shall enjoy the search,' Vita said.

'Then you only need a little warmth. I'll send a maid to light the fire directly.'

This seemed a great extravagance to Vita, brought up in a vicarage where economy was the first priority, but it didn't feel polite to resist Swain's generous offer. 'Thank you,' was all she said.

'It's good to see the library in use, Miss,' he replied, 'normally it has few visitors. Only Miss Hartley, the children's governess. You may meet her, but she reads only from the literature shelves over on the other side. Poetry, I believe is her chief interest. She will not interrupt you.'

*P*emberton Hall's famous round tower was briefly bathed by a pale sun. Its butter-coloured stonework glowed.

The two ladies at the drawing room window were watching younger people strolling along the garden walk below; a couple and a younger girl, taking advantage of a brief respite in the weather. The pair were in close conversation, absorbed and moving slowly. The girl ran and darted around them, dashing ahead, looping back, walking backwards to tell them something, then running forward again. Around them the sky softened into chalky smears of cloud underlit with lavender.

'Mary-Ann is like a puppy!' her mother said. 'She adores Lotti. She follows them wherever they go. She wants her hair like Lotti's, her dress like Lotti's. Lotti this, Lotti that. I suppose she has lacked an older sister growing up. I had never considered it before. Chaperoning suits her.'

'And what do you make of Lotti?'

Lady Pemberton turned and walked back to the fire. 'I have never in all my life seen a young man so entirely smitten. My son can hardly bear to be apart from her. If she so much as leaves a room he pines until she returns. It seems excessive to me, but perhaps a mother is not the best judge. Her family has great wealth and position, so it is a good match in one way. But we shall see so little of Alexander, once they marry. He already spends a great deal of time travelling.'

She stopped speaking and glanced suddenly over at her friend. 'Vita looks well. Is she staying with you for long?'

'I hope so. My brother takes his daughter too much for granted. She helps him in the parish and acts as his secretary in his natural history work. I suspect he has neglected her education because he finds her so useful.'

'She was a long time nursing her poor mother, as I recall.'

'Yes, she was a great comfort, but it has cost her several years of her youth. And she has been far too much alone. My brother did not think to include her in even the limited social life around them in Devon. I hope a stay in Cambridge will bring her out into the world a little.'

Lady Felicity touched her friend's arm. 'It will, Louisa, I'm sure. It's such a pleasure to have you to talk to, my dear. Can you spare the time from your college portrait commissions?'

'On that subject, I have a suggestion,' Louisa said. 'Why don't I make a little watercolour portrait of Alexander and Karlotta? Something quite modern and informal. It will capture the moment far better than a photograph – you know how stiff portrait photographs can be.'

'A portrait by you is always a delightful idea. Lotti's image is everywhere, but I shall have no portrait of Alexander if he marries and moves away.'

'Then I shall suggest the idea to Alexander as soon as I

see him. You haven't mentioned Dickie. How is his health recently?'

'He seems well enough. I see so little of him.'

'You do not spend time together?'

'He has a new valet. Billings. Billings was his old army batman, they served together. Dickie employed him a few months ago without consulting me. He has been very good for Dickie in many ways. He has instituted a daily routine and regular exercise and treatments. Dr Mills advises and Billings makes sure that every recommendation is followed to the letter. There is the possibility of real progress, apparently. With perseverance, Dickie might even be able to walk independently again.'

'All that sounds highly beneficial.'

'It is. Except I, as his wife, have no part to play. Billings rules over every detail of Dickie's existence. He has turned Dickie's dressing room into a sick room which I am hardly permitted to enter. When I do seem my husband, Billings is always there in the background. He lurks. He listens. Nothing must disrupt the patient's routine. The other staff dislike him. He is high-handed and unpleasant to the maids, but Dickie will not hear a word against him.'

'Does this concern you, Felicity?'

Felicity shrugged. 'Dickie's health is improving. He is stronger and complains less of pain. He sleeps well. I must be grateful for that.'

'And how will Dickie react to the engagement, if it is put to him?'

'I really can't say. He seems so remote from everyday life. He and Billings are in a separate world. I am not needed. I envy you your art, Louisa. It must be a fine thing to have your own occupation. Your own gift.'

'But you paint well yourself, Felicity. I remember

29

carrying easels to the cliffs to make seascapes in our girlhood. Do you have time nowadays?'

The lady of the house waved a hand, taking in high windows, ancient portraits, chandeliers and rugs on a marble floor stretching far into the distance. 'This house leaves little time for painting. Besides, I always preferred a walk in the fresh air to an afternoon in the studio, which is why my paintings are in the attic and yours hang in colleges and galleries! Shall we visit the stables while the rain holds off? There is still time to see Merriman's lovely new foal, if we hurry.'

As the two ladies threw on cloaks and bonnets, a dark-clothed woman approached. She moved silently, fluidly, as though hovering.

'I wonder if I might ask you something, Your Ladyship?' she said.

'Could it wait, Miss Hartley? We were on our way to the stables.'

'Of course,' said Miss Hartley, inclining her head and moving away so smoothly that she was gone before the sound of her mistress's words faded.

'Did Miss Hartley need something?' Louisa asked, as they stepped outside and took the stairs that curved towards the gardens.

'It will be Mary-Ann and the party again. My daughter is developing all sorts of unsuitable ideas. May she lengthen her dress? May she wear her hair up? And she sends poor Hartley running to me every five minutes with her requests. Or Miss Hartley sends herself. It is trying, frankly, when there is such an important occasion to prepare for.'

'Poor Hartley,' Louisa said, following her friend down the winding stone steps, 'a governess is always betwixt and between. Perhaps she is hoping for a chaperone's invitation for herself.'

They had reached the path in front of the house, heading for the stable block. Lady Felicity stopped abruptly and looked round at her friend. 'The thought never entered my head. Hartley has never dined with the family on formal occasions.'

'The children are growing. Hartley will soon have no Pemberton children left to educate. She may see it as her last chance to attend a gala occasion here at the Hall. And she is musical. She began the children's musical education, did she not? She would surely enjoy the concert.'

'Perhaps she would,' Lady Pemberton turned and strode away, 'but I have far more important matters to consider than a nervy governess's delusions of grandeur.'

CHAPTER 10

*V*ita walked back to the far corner of the library near the tall windows and pulling a volume of anatomy from the shelf, settled at one of the smaller tables and began to examine the contents: page after page of intricate illustrations of the complex layers of equine muscle, skin and bone. She was so absorbed that she jumped when she saw a figure had entered and was examining the shelves at the other end of the library.

The lady wore a brown dress. Indeed with dark hair and shawl she seemed sombre from head to toe. She looked pale, Vita noticed, and her arm, as it stretched to reach a high shelf, was thin enough for the sleeve to slide up at the wrist. Vita had a vague sensation of having seen her before. She watched as the lady, standing on tiptoe, first hunted hurriedly for something almost beyond her grasp, then located what she was seeking, and lifted down a small blue bottle. She looked relieved.

Vita felt that she ought, at this moment, to make her presence known. Not to do so would be rude. But she hesitated to interrupt the brown lady's anxious activity, settling for clearing her throat to show she was there.

This made the other lady start. In her shock she dropped several coins which must have been in her other hand. They rolled in all directions and she stooped to gather them in jerky movements. Vita quickly came across to help, but the coins were already retrieved. As she stood up the lady in brown seemed deliberately to change her expression from one of flustered anxiety to something more composed.

'We have not been introduced. I am the children's governess, Ada Hartley,' she said and held out a lace-gloved hand. 'You must be Mrs Brocklehurst's niece, Vita? I heard you were to join us. The children are eager to meet you.'

Her words were proper and welcoming, but Vita found Miss Hartley's hand cold and soft. It was a memorably unpleasant handshake.

'I am looking forward to meeting the children. Will they join the party at luncheon? Or perhaps I could visit them in the nursery?' Vita said.

This idea did not seem to appeal to Miss Hartley in the least. 'They will eat luncheon with their cousins. Mary-Ann will be attending the concert and dining with the guests this evening. It is her first adult dinner party and she is quite beside herself with excitement, as you can imagine.'

Vita couldn't really imagine being over-excited at the thought of a dinner party, but she smiled as if she could. It was only several minutes after the governess had left that Vita saw a silver sixpence on the rug where Miss Hartley must have dropped it. Vita picked it from the floor and put it into her pocket, thinking she would return it to the governess in person.

SHE HAD BARELY CAUGHT her breath before the doors opened again and an elegantly dressed young woman slipped into the library. She remained just inside, peering out into the corridor with her back to Vita, then danced lightly into the room, seeming delighted. It was only then that she saw that she was not alone.

'Oh! Someone is here!' she cried, in German.

'Pardon me,' Vita replied, in the same language, 'I was just exploring the library.'

'The girl stepped forward, 'You are one of the guests, I imagine. I am Karlotta Von Diepentahl.'

'Vita Carew. Delighted to meet you. I have heard a great deal...'

At this point, an elegant young man came quietly into the library, looking back out of the door behind him before turning with a look of delight to Karlotta. 'Ah, Lotti, at last! I couldn't escape!'

His expression changed to one of surprise and perhaps even disappointment, when he saw that she was already in conversation with Vita.

'We were just introducing ourselves, Alexander.'

The young man recovered his manners immediately. 'So I see.' He stepped forward and shook hands with Vita himself. 'You must be Mrs Brocklehurst's niece. Vita, isn't it?'

'Your aunt is a great artist, I believe,' Lotti said.

'She is certainly kept busy with her commissions,' Vita agreed.

'I should so love to have my portrait made by her!' Lotti said, 'I think somehow a lady painter would have a particularly delicate touch. Don't you think, Alexander?'

Alexander smiled indulgently at Lotti, but spoke to Vita. 'I heard that you are studying, Vita. Perhaps we are keeping you from your books?' He looked towards the desk where Vita had been reading.

'I was just exploring the library,' she told him. The pair, standing closely side by side both smiled kindly, but suddenly Vita felt again that it would be better if she left. 'I must see whether my Aunt needs me, if you'll excuse me now.'

'We are not driving you out, I hope,' Alexander said, still smiling.

'Not at all, I am expected.'

Vita gathered her book. Reaching the door, she heard Alexander say something quietly in German to Karlotta. He had already stepped closer to her.

'Vita *speaks German*, Sweetheart,' she heard Lotti reply quietly.

It was, Vita thought, as she climbed the stairs, an unchaperoned moment that she had interrupted. The quiet library - not quiet for very long, a maid was already approaching to light the fire - probably offered a rare opportunity for them to speak alone. At least one other person - a younger sibling or an older lady would always be present at meetings of a single lady and a gentleman. Propriety demanded it. Vita was old enough to have heard friends bemoan the inescapable chaperone. She might have felt embarrassed, but she was still turning over in her mind the odd encounter with Miss Hartley. She looked at the book in her hand and saw she had carried Venner's *Studies in The Anatomy of the Horse* away with her. Unexpected bed-time reading, but, ah well, the anatomy of the horse it would have to be. She would take it to her bedroom, she thought, only then realising that she did not know how to find the Yellow Bedroom.

he brisk figure of the housemaid led Vita up a wide staircase and across a landing which led onto a long hall hung with family portraits. Rain was falling once more outside the tall windows. As they approached the far end, a small group of children ran in and two boys began playing hide-and-seek, twisting themselves into the long curtains and crawling under sofas. Two older girls sat on one of the sofas, distancing themselves from the boys. The girls came over when they saw Vita.

'You must be Vita,' the younger of the two girls said. 'I am Mary-Ann. This is my cousin Virginia. These are our brothers, William is the one under the curtain. Oliver is under the sofa.'

The boys, now curious, extracted themselves from their hiding places and came over. They shook hands politely with Vita.

'Where are you going?' William asked the maid.

'I am showing Miss Carew to the Yellow Room, Master William.' She seemed eager to keep moving. I am interrupting her duties, Vita thought.

'We can show her, can't we Oliver?' William said. He took Vita's hand, so as to guide her. 'The Yellow Room is near the nursery.'

Vita was happy to agree.

The figure of the maid swiftly receded, leaving her to the attentions of the two little boys. The girls had already settled themselves back on the sofa, deep in conversation.

She was led away, up a further wooden staircase and through another door.

'It is quite easy to become lost in this house,' Oliver told her, as they walked.

'*I* never get lost,' said William, 'this way, Miss Carew'.

'You live here. Of course you don't get lost,' said his cousin. 'To visitors it is very complicated. There are so many staircases. My father says it is because of the fires.'

'The fires were a long time ago,' William said, opening a large door which led to another long passageway.

'Yes, but they changed the building after the fires,' his cousin insisted. 'It was to make it safer, but it also made it more complicated.'

They passed a full suit of armour standing to attention, and for some reason the boys both saluted it.

'That is the hero's armour,' William said, 'we always salute when we pass. You can too, if you like. It brings good luck.'

Vita rose to the challenge and gave the suit of armour her own formal salute. This won the boys' approval.

Along the chilly corridor they went, then across another landing and into another passageway. Here the walls were bare of paintings and there was a definite smell of damp. The corridor would have led off into the distance, but was blocked only a few feet beyond the first door by a very large mahogany tallboy placed across it.

'Here we are. This is your room,' William told Vita. He opened the first door on the left and both the boys ran into the Yellow Room. They ran to the windows and looked out at the rain.

'Thank you for bringing me here, William and Oliver,' Vita said. 'I am only worried now that I won't be able to find my way back.'

William came over. 'It's very easy really. There are four main staircases and this room is off the fourth one.'

'It's the one with the monkey picture at the foot of the stairs,' Oliver added. 'That's how I always remember.'

'The schoolroom and nursery are just above here,' William said, 'look, I'll show you the staircase, it's hidden.'

They led her back out of her room into the broad corridor. On the wall opposite the Yellow Room a very inconspicuous door was cut into the panelling. Only when you knew it was there could you see a small handle. William opened it and pointed up a flight of narrow twisting stairs. 'These are the servants' stairs, really, but they're quicker. My room and Mary-Ann's are up there. Shall we go up, Ollie? I can show you my new soldiers.'

After a hurried but polite goodbye, the boys ran off up the stairs. Vita could still hear their voices above as she retreated to the Yellow Room and looked around.

It was a grand room and very cold despite having two large ornate fireplaces. The curtains and wallpaper were all in yellow and gold, but even in the middle of the day the light was dim. There was a tang of mildew in the air.

It was certainly an example of the finest decoration of an earlier century, lavishly decorated from carpet to painted ceiling, but Vita did not find her bedroom at Pemberton Hall particularly welcoming. Her clothing and books had been unpacked by maids, so she found her nightdress looking familiar but completely out of place on the pillow of the over-poweringly draped and magnificent bed. So sumptuously canopied, so trimmed, flounced, gathered, embroidered, gilded and worked with emblems and coats of arms was this bed, that it seemed exactly the kind of bed Napoleon or indeed the Sun King himself would have felt at home in. Its mattress stood almost waist high, and peering under the tented canopy Vita could make out four chubby gilded angels looking down at the pillow from each inner corner. They were blank-eyed and woodworm had pocked their faces.

Having brushed her hair and straightened her dress - she could not change for she had no other day dress to change into - Vita was wondering whether she should go and find her aunt, when a soft knock on the door heralded the arrival of a housemaid. This one carried a coal bucket.

'I am to draw the curtains and lay the fire, Miss. Shall I put the light on?'

The maid walked to window and reached down to switch on the room's single electric lamp. A circle of soft light made the shadows darker in the corners.

'We have aired this room, but it is not often used,' the maid said. 'I will light the fire at tea time and there will be a warming pan in the bed tonight. There are more blankets in the lower drawers.'

'Why is this fireplace used and the other one not?' Vita asked.

'Those chimneys were changed years ago, Miss. They are blocked off now to stop the wind and the noise carrying from upstairs. Children can sometimes be noisy.'

'It seems a very splendid room to be so rarely used,' Vita said.

'The rooms beyond are not yet repaired, Miss. That is why the passageway is blocked. Will there be anything else?'

CHAPTER 12

*A*fter the maid had left, Vita studied the illustrated anatomy of the horse for a few minutes and then remembered Miss Hartley's sixpence in her pocket. The running footsteps and calls of William and Oliver playing on the floor above had stopped, but she could still hear some movement - adult footsteps on the wooden floor. Thinking it might be Miss Hartley, Vita left her room and opened the door to the hidden nursery staircase. She immediately heard voices from above. They sounded irritable enough to stop her with her foot on the bottom stair. The voice she heard first was Miss Hartley's.

'I left it exactly as usual,' she said. 'You have no business coming here.'

'It was sixpence short,' an angry male voice interrupted. 'You've had the goods.'

'I left the sum we agreed.' Miss Hartley was trying to keep her voice low. She spoke in a panicky whisper. It was this suggestion of secretiveness that prevented Vita going straight upstairs.

'It was short. I'm not doing this for the fun of it. I have to make special trips to that pharmacist, and you know this is a stronger mix than what is properly allowed. Gadd's taking a risk, so am I. We agreed a price. I only add a little extra for my trouble. I want what's due to me. I'm needed downstairs. I haven't the time to come chasing after you. Just leave the rest in the library by five. Don't keep me waiting, Ada, or there'll be trouble.'

'I am not able to pay you at present. I have not had time to make – to make arrangements.' Miss Hartley's tone was tinged with desperation.

'What arrangements? Sell something? Pawn something? Whatever you do, Ada, the money's owing. There'll be no more until you pay up.'

'Please, Billings. A day or two is all I ask. Without it I cannot sleep. The pain is unendurable.'

'We agreed terms. No more until I have what you owe.'

WITH A CLATTER OF BOOTS, the man started down the stairs. Vita fled across the passage and into the Yellow Room. The angry steps passed close. When she dared peer round the door, Vita saw a tail-coated figure step through the space between the cupboard that blocked the corridor and the wall. It was only wide enough for him to pass through sideways. He disappeared into the gloom of the dark passageway beyond, his footsteps loud on the bare boards.

Puzzled by this exchange, and worried that the sixpence in her pocket might be something to do with the argument, Vita decided to take it immediately to Miss Hartley and climbed the nursery stairs herself, calling Miss Hartley's name when she reached the floor above. She called several times before a door was opened and Miss Hartley, appeared, her expression unwelcoming.

'Miss Carew. The children are not here, as you can see.'

'I came to bring this. You dropped it in the library. I found it after you had left.'

Miss Hartley flinched. Her eyes fixed on the sixpence. She took it quickly, but seemed more irritated than grateful and said nothing, only looking back at Vita with something like suspicion.

At this moment the gong for luncheon rang through the house, giving Vita a good reason to hasten away.

Venturing back the way the boys had brought her was less easy than it might have been. She passed the suit of armour, but then could not remember whether it was near the second or the third staircase. One set of stairs seemed less carpeted and had no paintings. Vita followed it down until she reached the flagstones of a wide basement passageway, which led an impressive distance in either direction, running from one end of the house to the other.

She soon realised she had trespassed into the underground area of the great house; the domain of the servants. A bell rang nearby, making Vita jump and she could hear hurrying footsteps. The smells of a kitchen hard at work were distinct and voices were calling instructions. She was about to retreat when a gentleman in a smart uniform appeared beside her. It was the same man she had seen arguing with Miss Hartley.

'Lost your way, Miss?' he asked. 'It's easily done. You'll be looking for the dining room. Follow me.' He led her briskly along the flagstoned passage to the next staircase and up to the hall and dining room above.

How strange, she thought later, that one servant could make it appear such a pleasure to help a guest, and another, such as this man, without a word or an obvious gesture, could convey nothing but contempt and irritation.

CHAPTER 13

*V*ita counted thirty-two place settings at the dining table for luncheon. Hers was between Karlotta's German aunts, Tante Gabrielle and Tante Adelina: Gabrielle a fulsome presence and Adelina a tiny woman, anxious and twittery.

Gabrielle explained immediately that she was hard of hearing, 'I will hear you only if you speak loudly!' she called.

'She will hear you only if you speak loudly and slowly also,' Adelina added.

It was a light luncheon because a grand dinner was ahead of them, and Lady Pemberton had explained that it would be quite informal, but it was difficult to feel informal when served by footmen, and the courses kept coming. Soup was followed by fish, then meat and vegetables.

'I do not care for the manner of cooking meat in England,' Gabrielle remarked. 'It is not seasoned. I find it a little insipid. Is it always served in this manner?'

Vita felt unprepared for this subject in German or any other language. She had never travelled, so had no idea whether German beef tasted different from the English variety. It seemed undiplomatic either to agree or disagree. Luckily Gabrielle moved on from the topic.

'My bedroom has a very fine vista. Does yours, Adelina?'

'It looks over the garden in this direction,' Adelina said, indicating the direction of the window behind her. I can see a small building, which I believe to be the stables and there are horses. It is agreeable.'

'My view is superior, I think. I can see the great avenue of trees. It goes straight to the horizon. The countryside is most flat, is it not?'

'Yes, this part of the country is famous for its lack of hills,' Vita agreed.

'I like hills better,' declared Gabrielle, poking something on her plate with her fork. 'At home we have hills and mountains with snow also.'

'Do you travel often with your niece?' Vita asked.

'When she is making a tour of concerts we accompany her always. We have done this since she was a child. She was a child prodigy, you know. Always a great favourite. Usually we tour in Germany, but we have been to France and to Austria also. She has done this for many years. She is greatly celebrated and admired in these places.'

'So you are seasoned travellers,' Vita said.

Gabrielle shrugged, 'We have been to many cities where there are cultivated people who enjoy fine music.'

'We have not been to England before, however,' Adelina put in.

'The public is not musical in England,' Gabrielle remarked.

'Gabrielle, that is somewhat harsh!'

'Karlotta is hardly known here. In Paris or Vienna we could hardly pass in the train without people lining up to wave at her. Think of the reception we had at Strasburg in the spring. Here we travel almost incognito. The English are not musical people. Dear Prince Albert brought music and culture, which made a big improvement, but he is lost to us long ago, poor man.'

'My sister is a little quick to judge,' Adelina said to Vita in a quiet aside. 'She has not been sleeping well. The beds in London were not comfortable. Also we feel cold so often. Even here at Pemberton Hall. English houses have such drafts, do they not?'

Across the table, Vita noticed a very small, neat gentleman fastidiously separating food on his plate.

'You have met Dr Zecker? He is our personal physician. He travels with us all the time. Such a comfort.' Adelina smiled along the table to the doctor, who nodded courteously in reply. Vita watched him wave away a footman wielding a platter of beef. 'Dr Zecker *ist Vegetarier*,' Adelina said quietly.

Vita had heard of people being vegetarian, but had never met one. By the look of it neither had the other diners or the staff, who offered him meat several more times as the meal progressed.

'Do you know Alexander Pemberton well?' Gabrielle asked Vita.

'Not personally. My aunt is his Godmother, and is very fond of him, but I did not live with her until recently, so I have not met him before.'

'But you live now with your aunt?' Adelina asked, smiling approval at the idea of living with aunts in general.

'Yes, she is the lady over there speaking to Lady Pemberton.'

'Such a terrible thing. Lord Pemberton being crippled,' Gabrielle said loudly. 'He must suffer a great deal of pain. I know what it is to live with pain, do I not, Adelina?'

'I'm sorry to hear that,' Vita said, feeling some such comment was needed.

'I never sleep. There is almost no bed I can bear to lie on. If it were not for Dr Zecker I truly believe I should have perished for pain and lack of sleep many years ago. He is a miracle worker.'

'A miracle worker, truly,' Adelina agreed.

'Shall we let little Vita in on our secret?' Gabrielle suddenly asked. Despite her comments on the beef she had cleared her plate and was now contemplating a delicate pink jelly set trembling before her.

'Why not?' Adelina said. Both aunts looked suddenly thrilled.

CHAPTER 14

*G*abrielle leaned closer to Vita and announced in a penetrating stage whisper, 'We believe that our darling Karlotta and Alexander are to become engaged tonight. They will announce it after the concert.'

Vita could tell that awed excitement was required, and did her best to provide it. 'Really? Is this a great surprise to the rest of the company?'

'It is!' Adelina said, delighted. 'We tell you in the strictest confidence. Nobody else must know!'

'Oh, of course,' Vita agreed. 'And what are your feelings about this?' she asked, hardly daring.

Gabrielle paused to savour a mounded spoonful of jelly. She nodded briefly before answering. 'We approve. It was not easy. Our darling girl is such a treasure to us. We have raised her, you see. We have been with her since her earliest days and nurtured her gifts for many years, have we not, Adelina?'

'Yes, indeed. Nurtured them,' her sister agreed.

'But Alexander has won us over,' Gabrielle continued. 'Such a fine young man. So handsome, and such a musician! Of course, in our secret hearts - you will understand this

Fräulein Carew - in our secret hearts we had wished our darling to marry a German gentleman. That is only natural.'

'Only natural, yes,' Adelina said, nodding.

'But Alexander has overcome even those reservations. He has won our hearts as well as the heart of our darling Lotti.'

Both aunts looked indulgently down the table towards Alexander, who was in conversation with his neighbours, but he caught their eye and smiled back.

'Alexander understands Lotti's life. He knows that she must live for her music,' Gabrielle concluded, reaching to spoon another jelly onto her plate and adding a whirl of sweetened cream. 'He will not make any difficulties. Everything will continue as before.'

'Yes,' agreed her sister, 'everything will be *exactly* as before.'

Exactly as before? Surely not? Vita thought vaguely, but a happy silence ensued, during which further dazzling desserts – gateaux, tarts, mousses, jellies and ices continued to be carried to the table. Dr Zecker, she noticed, chose an apple from a sumptuous pyramid of more exotic fruit, and peeled it with absolute precision before slicing it into wafers and eating it with a knife and fork. From the other end of the table came gales of laughter, which mainly seemed to be prompted by a gentleman Vita did not recognize, seated next to Karlotta.

'That Italian gentleman is the great Signor Ricci,' Aunt Adelina told Vita.

Vita was none the wiser. He was a smiling, moustachioed gentleman, fully engaged in charming the other end of the table. His accented voice rang out above the general conversation.

'He is an *impressario*!' Gabriella said.

Vita hesitated to ask what this was. She did not want to

appear ignorant when his presence alone seemed to thrill the German ladies so.

'He has travelled especially from London to hear Karlotta sing today. A great honour. If he is impressed by her performance, he may engage her to sing at La Scala in Milan. This is the greatest opera house in the world. Greater, even, than the one in Vienna.'

'Nothing is certain, of course,' Adelina added. 'But if Karlotta sings in Milan it will bring her fame throughout the opera world. She richly deserves this, we believe. Very few sopranos can compare with her purity of tone.'

'Almost none,' agreed her sister, 'but Signor Ricci looks not only at the quality of the voice, but at the temperament of the singer. He told me this in person. This is why he is here tonight, to meet Karlotta and to see her in the heart of her family, so to speak.'

'Does having such an important guest make Karlotta nervous when she sings?' Vita asked.

Gabriella set her spoon aside with a sigh of contentment. 'Nervous? Oh no. Karlotta is always happy when she sings. She loses herself in her music. It has always been so. I am glad to see Signor Ricci is enjoying himself. A good meal is always helpful in the enjoyment of music.'

The aunts looked around the company contentedly for a few moments.

'Does the Lord Pemberton not eat with his guests?' Adelina asked Vita.

'I believe his health varies. He joins the table when he is able, but a place is always laid for him.'

'I understand. A great pity. We have not yet met Lord Pemberton, and, naturally, we are most eager to meet the father of our dear Alexander.'

Even as she spoke, the door opened and Lord Pemberton

was wheeled into the room. He took his place at the head of the table and began conversing amiably with guests on either side. At the far end of the table his wife smiled a welcome. The conversation, which had paused at his arrival, resumed.

'Father and son look very alike, do they not?' Adelina remarked, quietly. 'Both very handsome men, and the Lord is very strong-looking, even in his chair.' She sounded approving.

But Tante Gabrielle was not so easily won round. 'He has the complexion of a soldier - a little too much of the sun, I think. It is harsh on the fair skin. It increases the *Sommersprossen*. How do you say this in English?'

Vita, put suddenly on the spot, struggled with the unfamiliar German word. It seemed to mean Summer-*something*, but she couldn't guess what.

'I believe he served in Africa,' Tante Adelina continued.

'Is this where he was injured?' asked her sister.

'It was a riding accident, I believe.'

'He is a handsome man. His bone structure is very good,' Gabrielle declared, 'we must forgive him a few *Sommersprossen*.'

Alexander again beamed a smile at the aunts, and both give him little waves in return. He stood and came over.

'Did you enjoy the dessert, Tante Gabrielle? I asked especially for strawberry jelly. Your favourite.'

'You remembered!' she said, delighted.

'Of course! I asked Chef especially. We want you to feel quite at home, here. And you too, Adelina.'

Both ladies glowed with delight at this attention.

'And Miss Carew, thank you for your translating and making our German guests feel welcome,' he added in English, turning to focus his charming smile on Vita this time. 'I believe your brother is at Trinity now. Reading...was it Natural Sciences?'

'Yes, Edward is about to begin his second year,' Vita said.

'And you are staying with your aunt? Is that to study art?'

'Well, I am rather more interested in science than art.'

'Science? How unusual,' Alexander remarked, but his attention had been caught by movement at the end of the table.

He immediately made excuses to the ladies, and walked across to take the handle of his father's wheelchair so that father and son could leave together.

The man who had wheeled Lord Pemberton in, Vita noticed, stood watching with signs of protective concern as his lordship was wheeled away. Then he remembered he was surrounded by guests and left swiftly by a side door. It was the same irritable man who had run down the nursery stairs and later escorted her to the dining room.

'Perhaps this is the moment he will speak to his father about our little secret,' Tante Adelina remarked in a low voice.

'I imagine so. Yes, this would be a good moment.' The aunts both suppressed gleeful excitement.

'I believe I heard you say you had an interest in science?' Adelina then asked, turning piercing blue eyes to study Vita.

'Yes. I try to follow my brother's course of study. I help him sometimes with his notes.'

'There are some women who become scientists,' Adelina remarked, 'in Germany this is so. German universities welcome all talented scholars, even women. My cousin's daughter is interested in mathematics. She is very advanced in her studies, I believe.'

'I am old-fashioned, perhaps' Gabrielle declared, 'but I have never believed in encouraging young women to study at

51

university. They should marry and have children as nature intended. Studying might perhaps be a pastime for older women, once their family is around them, but even then there are far more important occupations. Husbands are not easy to find for very intelligent women. Young men are not happy with young women who know more than they do. I was careful never to know more on any subject than my own dear husband.'

'How very thoughtful of you, Gabrielle,' remarked her sister, 'but Vita, I believe your aunt is trying to attract our attention.'

'In future,' said her aunt, as they left the dining room, 'just touch your left shoulder twice and I will come to the rescue. Were they hard work, the German aunts?'

'We were doing well enough until we got onto women studying science,' Vita said.

'I could see you needed help from the other end of the table, my Dear, but I don't think anyone else noticed. Will you join the company in the drawing room? Signor Ricci is very entertaining, I'll introduce you.'

'I need to look something up in the dictionary first. A German word,' Vita said.

'How diligent you are. Alexander and Lotti were very enthusiastic about having their portrait made. I mentioned it over luncheon just now. I shall start this afternoon. Join us for the first sitting when you can.'

Sommersprossen? The word stuck irritatingly in Vita's head. As soon as she could escape, she hurried to the library to look it up. She had no sooner lifted the heavy dictionary to a corner table and begun turning its pages, than the library door opened and Lord Pemberton's valet slipped inside. He glanced around, but did not wait to check the room thoroughly, stepping over and reaching up to a high shelf instead. Whatever he found there was slipped straight into his waistcoat pocket. Turning so fast the tails of his jacket flew behind him, he was gone, with only the slowly closing door to show he had been there.

It suddenly came to Vita that Miss Hartley, the woman who had stretched to reach that same high shelf and dropped a sixpence, was the same anxious woman she had seen buying medicine in the chemist's shop in Cambridge a few weeks before.

She found the word. Freckles. *Sommersprossen* meant freckles. *Of course!*

THE PORTRAIT SITTING was to take place in the long parlour. An easel had been set up near the great windows which curved around the circular turret overlooking the formal gardens.

Vita found the elderly German aunts waiting cheerfully on a sofa a few feet away.

'Come Vita, sit with us,' said Tante Gabrielle, patting the sofa between them. She wore her customary widow's black, down to her lace gloves and cap. The darkness of her gown was offset by the soft fineness of the silken fabrics, layered and pleated around her. Tante Adelina, who had never married, wore a lilac dress with lacework at the neck in a style that dated from many years before.

'I have never seen a portraitist at work. This is most delightful!' Tante Adelina said.

'Of course, Karlotta has had her portrait made already several times,' added Gabrielle. 'One of the portraits was commissioned by Grand Duke Frederick of Baden for his personal collection. It hangs in the musicians gallery at his palace, I have seen it there myself.'

'How proud you must be,' Vita said. It was a form of words she was finding useful with the aunts.

'She is a dear treasure to us,' Adelina put in, 'she always has been, has she not, Gabrielle?'

'Always, always. Nothing but a continual joy from her earliest years. A darling child, a beauty, and such talent, even as a baby.'

Vita smiled and looked across to where the chairs were being prepared for the sitters. She wondered whether it was only her own nature, or human nature in general, to feel dislike for anyone so endlessly and fulsomely praised. Karlotta was beautiful, she was talented, she was everybody's favourite of favourites, from the Grand Duke – and probably

Kaiser Wilhelm himself - to the lowliest footman who sprang eagerly to attention if she so much as glanced his way. It was only normal to feel a little irritation, surely?

Perhaps it is the English way of thinking, Vita thought, as Karlotta and Alexander arrived separately and with shows of modesty and good manners took their seats together. Or perhaps it is a deficiency in my own character, to suspect that continuous exposure to fawning adoration is not a good preparation for life.

Or perhaps, she thought, as the aunts settled themselves in anticipation on the sofa around her, it is simply envy that I feel. After all, no Grand Duke is ever likely to wish for *my* portrait.

'Your face could be quite attractive, if you wore your eyeglasses a little less, Vita,' Tante Gabrielle remarked, as if detecting Vita's own thoughts. 'I always think spectacles are best avoided, especially on a social occasion.'

And why, exactly, is it better to fall down the stairs or walk into furniture than be seen in glasses? Vita longed to ask, but the old lady was already exclaiming, 'What a couple they make! They are simply adorable! I only hope the artist has the skill she needs.'

'Is it true Vita, that Lotti first met Alexander at your aunt's home? This is what I heard,' asked Adelina.

'Yes, I believe that is true,' Vita told her. 'My aunt was painting a college portrait of your relative.'

'Yes, Max, our cousin, a very brilliant man, he is a professor,' Adelina said.

'Alexander had called on my aunt, he has known her since childhood, and met Karlotta when she came with the professor.'

'It must have been destiny that brought them together, both talented artists, both musicians. A match made in heaven!' Tante Gabrielle accepted a cup of coffee from a footman and sipped it happily, balancing the cup and saucer comfortably upon her prominent bosom. Her feet, which did not quite reach the ground, swung a little to and fro under her skirts, for joy.

'I am surprised not to see Lady Pemberton here,' Tante Adelina remarked, after the painting had been under way for a while. 'She would surely have enjoyed the sight of Lotti and Alexander being painted together.'

'English ladies often go horse riding every single day of the year,' her sister remarked. 'Perhaps she is galloping across the park!'

The thought made her shudder.

'I have heard such things also,' Adelina agreed.

'We had a neighbour in Bad Wirtesheim who rode her horse every day, Anna Maria Von Vurstemburg, do you remember?'

'Of course, she caught pleurisy one winter, it is only to be expected...'

...and so the ladies' talk continued. Vita had no need to translate, or pay particular attention, which gave her a few moments to think about the strange happenings in the library.

Some sort of exchange was obviously being transacted between the valet and Miss Hartley. She left money and collected a small bottle. But why was it all so secretive? And what gave the valet the freedom to speak so cruelly to her when he thought she had underpaid by sixpence? It was the same sort of bottle that Miss Hartley had bought that day from the dingy chemist. Medicine, clearly, but what sort of medicine? Something Miss Hartley had desperate need of, and found it difficult to pay for, it would seem.

It was just as she had reached this plateau in her thoughts that Vita noticed something had changed in her Aunt Louisa's demeanour. Louisa had been making preliminary sketches, using pencil, working swiftly and silently, having carefully arranged the couple so that the light fell across their faces in the way she preferred. Vita had often seen her aunt at work and enjoyed it. The artist's absorption and the way it took her out of her surroundings to focus only on capturing the shapes and colours that added up to a likeness was fascinating to observe.

Aunt Louisa, in her favourite apron, much worn and stained with paint, had next mixed watercolours in a palette, and laid on a wash for either face. Now and again she paused, stepped back, looked searchingly towards the couple as if checking something, then moved back to the paper and added another few deft brushstrokes.

The aunts continued to speak in low tones. Footmen came and went with refreshments.

Then, quite suddenly, Vita sensed a change in her aunt's bearing. Louisa stood back from her easel. For a fraction of a moment a look of irritation seemed to cross her face, but was immediately replaced with a smile. Her shoulders relaxed.

'This needs to dry. For now my dears, you are free to go.'

'And we may look at the painting?' Lotti asked, leaning a little forward.

'I would rather you waited,' the artist told her.

Lotti made a little pout with her mouth, but then laughed her lightest laugh and turned to Alexander. 'In that case, we should rehearse. I should like to run through the second song in particular, but first there are my voice exercises to do. Could you play for me in the library, Tante Adelina?'

'Of course, my dear,' called her aunt.

'Shall I join you in half and hour?' asked Alexander.

'Yes, that would be perfect.'

*B*y mid-afternoon a few younger people were still taking the air in the gardens, or finishing a match in the billiard room, but more experienced guests were in their rooms, resting. As Louisa and Vita made their way upstairs, Louisa pointed out familiar landmarks: the suit of armour; the long case clock; the sweeping curves of the central staircase with its rows of family portraits.

Louisa knew the house well. 'I always have the sense,' she told Vita, as they walked along the landing, 'of generations of people flowing like water between these ancient stones and timbers. A house like this has seen so many people come and go and will far outlast us all. Oh look, Vita! Here is the Admiral. My favourite!'

Near the staircase she paused to admire a full length study of one of the Pemberton ancestors in the manner of Sir Joshua Reynolds. Wearing an expression of composed superiority, the gentleman stood with one hand upon the curving surface of a large spherical model of the earth. The other hand gestured over his shoulder, where far in the background a small pair of galleons were doing battle, giving the viewer to understand that in his day he had been a brave sea warrior.

Louisa considered the sea captain an old friend, and loved the portrait for details that few others passing on the stairs were likely to observe. His cheeks were ruddy in the manner of someone whose life had been spent on the high seas. They matched exactly the colour of his splendid waistcoat, a gold-embroidered garment falling in scarlet beneath a naval jacket.

He was a gentleman whose figure suggested that he had eaten well since retiring from the sea, and it was Louisa's particular joy to notice, whenever she passed, that the portraitist had captured the strain being suffered by each of the gilded buttons across his generous stomach - the curve of which precisely echoed that of the globe beside him. Best of all, a single button appeared to have given up the battle and come undone, so that just at his waist the scarlet silk gaped to reveal a glimpse of white linen below. The texture of his blue velvet jacket, the highlights on its gold brocade: Louisa admired the work as only a fellow portraitist could.

She was leaning on the banister, pointing out the delicate detail of the seaman's plump left hand, when she and Vita both noticed a figure pass swiftly across the hall beneath and turn towards the lesser staircase that led to the kitchens. It was Miss Hartley.

There was no particular reason why the governess should not be about at this time, but something caused the ladies to look questioningly at each other.

'I wonder what Miss Hartley is doing. She has not been herself recently, I'm told,' Louisa said.

'Perhaps she has business in the kitchens.' Vita looked over the bannister. 'Should I follow?' The suggestion was only half serious, but Louisa nodded.

'Felicity has said one or two things about Miss Hartley

that are slightly alarming. We would not want anything to disturb this evening's grand event. Just follow her discreetly and see what she is about. I shall wait here.'

Vita hurried down, crossed the landing below and took the lower flight of stairs after the governess. Miss Hartley entered the servants' basement corridor, turned left and opened a small side door. She was in and out in an instant and turned back towards the stairs, but Vita saw her draw an envelope from her pocket as she entered. As she stepped out again, her hand was sliding something into the same pocket. The governess seemed intent, walking rapidly with her eyes downcast, oblivious to her surroundings. She continued along the corridor towards the great kitchens at the end. Vita followed, noting as she passed it that the door the governess had opened was labelled *Chef*.

From the kitchen at the far end of the long passageway came cheerful voices and the sounds of a meal in preparation. Miss Hartley, with her silent, gliding walk, went in. The voices stopped, as if her presence had been noted. No greeting followed. It seemed to Vita that Miss Hartley's visit to the kitchen was unwelcome.

Feeling out of place herself, Vita went back upstairs, waiting near the dining room doors to see whether Miss Hartley would leave the kitchens a different way. After a few moments, she did appear.

'Ah, Miss Hartley,' Vita said.

The governess looked startled, but recovered enough to say, 'It is always a wonderful sight, the table being prepared before a dinner begins. The dining room with all the flowers and the silverware - it never looks quite as perfect when it is crowded with people.' She gestured towards the dining room where a team of footmen were at work.

'Indeed,' Vita said, and stood beside Miss Hartley to look into the dining room.

'I do not care for crowds,' Miss Hartley continued, 'I prefer to dine alone, as a rule. But I should dearly have loved to hear the concert. She is a fine soprano, you know, Miss Von Diepentahl. I have read about her often. She is much praised. Opera is a particular passion of mine.'

'Will you not attend the concert?'

'I am not … not to be a guest tonight,' Miss Hartley said.

There was pain in this answer. Vita struggled to know how to react. 'I suppose if you dislike large gatherings…'

'I taught Alexander music when he was a boy, you know. It was I who gave him his very first lessons; singing and piano. Nurtured his talent. Of course he soon outgrew my limited skills, but I like to think I sowed the seeds. I could never have imagined he would one day perform all over Europe with someone as celebrated as Miss Diepentahl, but I always felt he would make his mark in the world of music. He has a natural gift.'

This speech seemed to exhaust Miss Hartley. She sighed and then turned sharply to Vita. 'Miss Carew, you have shown me kindness. You took the trouble to return the coin I had left in the library. Will you allow me to give you one small piece of advice?'

Vita nodded, wary of the governess's brittle intensity. Ada Hartley looked back into the dining room where a towering floral arrangement was being lifted onto a side table by a pair of footmen.

'You are a young woman with your life ahead of you, but like me you are not from a wealthy family. If anyone ever suggests you become a governess, I advise you to resist it with every force you can muster. Your affections, your energies and such talents as you may have will be drained from you like rain from a gutter and you will be left like me: sick, unwanted and despised.'

That said, the governess slid away, her gliding footsteps silent along the hall.

Vita was so taken aback by the governess's words that she stayed where she was. In the dining room, a row of tall silver candelabras had been placed along the table and the footmen were beginning to lay place settings, measuring the distance between them with a ruler. A portrait of the young Queen Victoria, solid in a dress of sky blue silk, watched sternly from above the fireplace as if scrutinising the work of Swain and his men. She did not look particularly impressed.

Turning to re-join her aunt, Vita noticed a swift movement at the far end of the hall. It was a tailcoated figure she recognised as Billings hurriedly climbing the stairs. Without pausing to think, Vita followed, curious to know why he was so often nearby when Miss Hartley was about.

At the white monkey portrait the boys had mentioned as a landmark, she lost sight of him, but met her aunt.

CHAPTER 17

*L*ouisa was studying another painting. 'Hardly anyone pays attention to the paintings,' she told Vita. 'If you live among them, they soon become invisible, no doubt. I like to imagine them waiting for me here, dear old friends, rather lonely and lacking attention between my visits.'

The stairway, though not grand, was handsome enough, lit from a skylight above. It turned two right angles, but with long treads and only a gentle rise on each step, so that it seemed to take many steps to make any upward progress.

'We shall examine this still-life,' Aunt Louisa declared. 'What do you make of it?'

The large canvas framed to one side of the staircase was a Dutch still-life. Vita had seen similar paintings, usually colourful vases of flowers and fruit tumbling towards the viewer. Occasionally she had also seen one which included game birds and joints of meat, also representing the bounties of nature and the delights of a well-stocked pantry. Here, though, the extravagance and generosity had tipped over into something different.

The first thing that caught the eye - the centrepiece, lit and standing out from a shadowy background - was a headless turkey placed so that its red wattled neck lay draped over a stone step. A few prettily painted grapes and peaches were beside it on the ground, but so was a dead peacock, its gorgeous tail feathers fanned out in the background. Closest to the front of the canvas, exactly at eye level to anyone climbing the stairs, were the sightless eyes of a dead cockerel lying on his back with his head at a nasty angle so that his beak and a few feathers almost touched a peach.

Off to one side, leering above the head of the viewer, was an odd little figure which turned out on examination to be a small white monkey, certainly alive, but appearing shocked and jabbering. It held its thin arms out at its sides and danced on one leg, its facial expression set in a silent shriek.

Vita hardly knew where to start. 'Well, I can see it's ...'

Her aunt was peering at the painting, looking delighted. 'What a monster! Really! I can hardly pass it without exclaiming! I must have seen it a hundred times, but its horror never ceases to make me tremble!'

'Is it a masterpiece, Aunt?' Vita asked, worried that she ought to know.

'Oh no, it's just a worthy old bit of Dutch nonsense, bought by the yard by a Pemberton ancestor, don't worry about that Vita. It has well-executed details - look at the grapes and the feathering on the birds - no, it's the outrageous arrogance of it that takes my breath away. Look, the setting is a temple and every detail in the background suggests gods and goddesses. The clear idea is that the place in the painting - if you look closely you can see it's Pemberton Hall - is heaven itself, awash with the bounty of nature. The owners are therefore gods and have been given all the creatures of the earth for their own greedy purposes.'

'Does that explain the monkey?'

'Yes, he is another of the creatures of the earth we have all been granted to do with as we wish, poor thing.'

'At least he has not been decapitated, like the poor turkey, or strangled like the peacock. Can you eat peacock?'

'Of course. It probably tastes like chicken, they usually do. Except swan, that tastes vaguely fishy.'

'You've eaten *swan*?'

'Years ago. They serve it at certain college feasts by special permission of the monarch. I would definitely not recommend it. Now, Dear, tell me about Miss Hartley. I was watching over the banister. You had quite a conversation.'

CHAPTER 18

*E*unice Parks, the housekeeper, had a comfortable private sitting room just off the kitchens. In one corner a door, to which only she held the key, led to the dry stores, where tea, sugar, salt, spices and other precious household commodities were kept. Her parlour, as befitted her seniority, was a spacious room. Although it was in the basement, the windows were only half below ground, and the view at the top was of the finest prospect Pemberton offered, a seemingly endless vista down a broad avenue of oaks and far off into the hazy distance of the wide flat landscape.

The fire was lit, its flames reflecting in the glaze of the larger china dishes stored in the dressers that encircled the walls. The room was warm and smelt of baking and the cloves and cinnamon stored nearby. Mrs Parks, a thin woman of a naturally stern bearing, kept the household accounts, writing entries in the ledger every evening in a curly copperplate hand. She had been at Pemberton for twenty-three years and no error had ever been found in her bookkeeping, but the fear of one still troubled her night and day. Apart from errors in the account books, which God forbid, the other two great fears of the housekeeper were fire and theft.

Fires had at one time been so regular at Pemberton Hall that it was now something the entire staff lived in continual vigilance against. Other households might occasionally forget a candle or light a careless torch in the stables, but no one here would do so.

Theft, on the other hand, was as likely to occur at Pemberton as in any other great house. That is to say, it was rare. When something precious went astray, the loss was usually due to carelessness rather than dishonesty.

A housekeeper's worst nightmare, of course, was the loss of a precious item, a piece of jewellery, for example, belonging to an important guest. Suspicion invariably fell on the servants. Eunice Parks had herself known of a case where a lost diamond brooch led directly to the dismissal of a ladies' maid, a butler and two footmen, even though the brooch was found in the lady concerned's handbag a short time later. Someone had to be made an example of in such cases, so that servants everywhere could learn the lesson.

For many years Eunice Parks's fervent prayers for the household she supervised to be spared the horror of theft had been granted by a kindly God, but in the past six months He had been less merciful and they had been bothered by the persistent loss of small items. Worry infiltrated Mrs Parks's dreams. She was convinced it was turning her hair grey.

The chef, smart in his white jacket, had accepted a cup of tea and a seat at her little dining table.

'Are you sure, Monsieur Picard?' she asked him. 'You haven't just misplaced them or lent them to someone?'

'Absolutely not. I have only a single pair. I hoped perhaps someone had handed them to you.'

'Where would they have been?'

'In my work room. Unless I am wearing them, I keep them there always. But now they are gone.'

Mrs Parks sighed. She was sitting upright and formal on a hard dining chair. 'Jeannie was cleaning there earlier,' she said.

'I have asked her already. She saw nothing on my table when she cleaned.'

'You have searched the room very thoroughly?'

'Yes. I am certain.'

The chef hesitated. He picked up his tea cup, but only looked into it without drinking. 'I have only one possible explanation.'

'Oh dear,' said Mrs Parks, for she could guess what he was about to tell her.

'It is the governess again.'

'But whyever should Miss Hartley steal your eyeglasses, Monsieur?'

'There is no reason. She has just begun, recently, to take things. Small things. She comes into my room. She comes sometimes into the kitchens and when she does, small things are missing.'

'You have noticed this before?'

'The small losses, yes. But I had not realised before what was happening. Now I see it. It is her. It is Miss Hartley. It must be her.'

'It is not like you to speak harshly about a lady,' Mrs Parks said.

'Mrs Parks,' the chef leant forward and lowered his voice, 'I believe she is a little mad.'

'I know she can be haughty...'

'Haughty?' the chef said, not seeming to know the word.

'Proud, you know, high and mighty, la-de-da.'

'Yes, she is, but it is more than that.' The chef frowned

and looked away as he continued. 'She decided that she wanted to be my close friend, you see. My special, particular friend.'

'Oh, did she?'

'I did nothing to encourage her, nothing at all.'

'Men often say that after the event, if I recall.'

The chef put his cup and saucer down on the table, still without taking any of the tea. He closed his eyes.

'Madame,' he said, quietly, 'you have known me for nearly ten years, I think.'

'I have.'

'And in that time, Madame, have I comported myself in any way improperly, in relation to any lady?'

'Improperly?' Mrs Parks raised an eyebrow and considered for a moment. 'Well, no.'

'Perhaps it is because I am a Frenchman and speak your language with an accent that everyone in England thinks I will be running after every female, young or old, who crosses the horizon, but the evidence is there to show you that this is not true.'

'I admit I have seen no sign of such behaviour, Monsieur Picard.'

'That is because there has *been* no such behaviour, Madame.'

'But Miss Hartley took it into her head that...'

'I once paused to listen to her playing the piano in the library, and Miss Hartley, for no reason other than that, decided I had strong feelings for her. I did not. I do not. I never said so. I never did anything to suggest it.'

'And that has led to her stealing your eyeglasses?'

'My eyeglasses this time. My favourite paring knife before, and one of my kitchen aprons before that.'

'Does Mr Swain know about this?'

'Yes. I have told him.'

'What did he say?'

'He said the other staff already talked about her in this connection. I did not know she had this reputation.'

'Yes. The maids have called her Miss Lightfingers for some time. She seems to have settled on your belongings now, but several small things have gone missing from the laundry and elsewhere.'

'It is intolerable. What can we do?'

'I cannot disrupt the great occasion tonight, Monsieur.'

'Of course not, Madame, but I have need of my eyeglasses. I cannot see to cook!'

'Mr Swain and Tom will go into her room and search for them.'

'I am most grateful.'

'Is all well, otherwise? With the dinner preparations, I mean?'

CHAPTER 19

'*N*ot again,' Tom said, 'what's she made off with this time?'

Swain, who had called the footman into the butler's pantry, was in his shirtsleeves and wearing a brown apron. He had laid the carving knives out on his table, running from one side to the other, from large to small, ready for sharpening. A task he always carried out before an important dinner.

Swain looked severely at the young man, disapproving of his tone, although he agreed wholeheartedly that it was an irritation to have small items disappearing. The staff were infuriated by it, which was bad enough, but what if she began lifting valuables? A governess was free to wander most rooms, she had only to take a beloved ornament or, God forbid, a purse or earring .... So far he had not broached the matter of Miss Hartley's stealing with the Mistress - she had far greater things to concern her - but he doubted this discretion could continue. Something would have to be said.

'Mr Picard has lost his eyeglasses.'

The footman uttered a loud bark of laughter, 'From off his nose, was it?'

'From his room, which is worse.'

'You mean she's prowling around people's rooms now?'

'If he's right, then yes.'

'I don't like the sound of that. We don't lock the doors. Upstairs on the men's side I don't think we've even got the keys.'

'Nobody likes the thought of a thief in their room. There have been... *difficulties* between the chef and Miss Hartley. I'd ask you to keep this to yourself, Tom. I don't want the maids worrying about this sort of thing when there's such a lot to be done.'

'No. Right you are,' Tom said. 'So what shall we do?'

'After the party is over and things are back to normal, I shall take further steps to put an end to all this, but until then, we will just pay Miss Hartley's room a quick visit. She walks the children to the stables at about this time.'

'I saw them go from the window.'

'Then I suggest we go upstairs immediately.'

The governess's rooms consisted of a small sitting room and a bedroom beyond. The men, having let themselves in, stood at first motionless in the centre of the sitting room, unsure of how to proceed. Nothing was out of place. The rooms were so extremely tidy that it was difficult to believe it was lived in at all.

'I'll look in those cupboards,' Tom said. 'She must have a trunk somewhere. Under the bed most likely.'

It felt even more intrusive than they had imagined. On principle Swain disliked having to look in Miss Hartley's private rooms - servants had little enough privacy - but groping under her bed and going through her trunk was almost too much for him to bring himself to do. Still, he found the trunk at the foot of the brass bedstead and opening it, he began to search. It contained only books, a dress which smelt of mothballs and a collection of small medicine bottles.

The bed, primly tucked in and covered in what looked like a flowery shawl, was as chilly-looking and lean, he thought, as Miss Hartley herself. Without thinking he put his hand on the thin pillow, and felt something odd. Moving it aside he saw a pair of silver-rimmed spectacles that were undoubtedly Monsieur Picard's. There was also a thin silver pencil, and a single shirt collar stud.

Swain called Tom to show him.

'Oh Gawd, she sleeps with his things under her pillow,' said Tom. 'She really is sweet on the old fellow.'

Swain put the items into his trouser pockets. 'We have what we wanted. I suggest we go.'

They both looked around.

'This place gives me the creeps,' Tom said. 'What's she going to say when she finds the stuff gone?'

'What can she say without admitting to theft?'

'She isn't quite right in the head, I reckon,' Tom said, waiting on the landing as Swain closed the door. 'Still at least the Frenchman will be able to read his menus again. Can't have him putting salt in the custard, poor old chap!'

It WAS SATISFYING, as least, to return the spectacles to the chef. Swain found him in the kitchen, in his whites, beating eggs for a sauce. Without a word he handed him the spectacles. The chef sighed in relief and put them on. The pencil and shirt stud he smiled at in recognition.

'These I had not even noticed,' he said, putting them into his pocket. 'Thank you, Monsieur Swain, you understand that I could not speak to her about this myself.'

'Yes. And I advise you not to in future, either,' said the butler. 'She will face the consequences, but I shall not say anything until after the party.'

'Of course,' said Monsieur.

'I pity her, Monsieur, between you and me, but we cannot allow this to continue.'

'She is wrong in the head, in my opinion,' Monsieur said. 'It is a kind of madness. It is called *cleptomanie* in French, in English I do not know the word. It is pitiful indeed.'

'Yes. I have come across such things once or twice, above stairs. It isn't usually given such a fancy name here below. They just call it thieving and send you up before the magistrates. Let's get the party over with, and then we can see what can be done about Miss Hartley.'

CHAPTER 20

$\mathcal{T}$he salon was aglow. Candlelight reflected on the gilded plasterwork of the ceiling, casting the softest light over every surface in the room. By day, the elaborate mouldings of swathed fruits and flowers looked cracked in places and a little shabby, but they were transformed by the light of the fires at either end of the long room and the chandeliers all along its length. This was Pemberton Hall at its grandest. The guests, in their finery, made a spectacle worthy of their elegant setting. The gentlemen in evening dress, the ladies in silks with feathered headpieces, pearls, diamonds, and tiaras. Rich floral perfumes of rose, honeysuckle, and jasmine filled the air, scenting the winter's night like a summer garden.

The two aunts were on a sofa near the front, when they saw Vita they patted a chair beside them to summon their interpreter to their side.

'Such a lovely dress, you have, Vita!' Tante Adelina whispered.

Gabriella agreed. 'Indeed yes,' she said, 'most suitable,

Miss Carew. Our German fashions are a little different, however.'

Alexander was already at the grand piano when Karlotta entered, spectacular in a rosy pink gown that fell low on her shoulders and trailed a lacy train behind. She was a different young woman now; a confident professional. With no sign of self-consciousness or hesitation she smiled and nodded briefly at the room, then took her place near the piano. Everyone sat forward with murmurs of expectation. Alexander played a brief introduction, and Karlotta Von Diepentahl began the first song.

Lotti's fine soprano was a revelation to Vita, who had sat through many evenings of singing to the piano at home in Devon. Her father's neighbours and friends loved a musical evening. Several of the ladies and one or two of the gentlemen farmers and other men of the church were fancied as having fine singing voices, but as she listened, Vita realised they were like sparrows to a nightingale. The singers Vita had heard before sounded musical and pleasant, some-times they even made the words of a song seem moving, but Lotti's singing reached into the listener's heart with a purity and power that was overwhelming. Vita was prepared for skill and mastery of technique - Karlotta was an esteemed singer with an international reputation, after all - but neither Vita nor the other English guests were prepared for the way the soprano's voice seemed to speak directly to their souls. Tears ran down many cheeks; in short it took only a few bars of the first song before the whole audience fell under the spell of a beautiful voice giving a great performance.

The servants, though not invited as guests, had an unusu-ally good view of the performance too. Pemberton had been altered a hundred years before. The famous architect had chopped rooms up, added stairways, raised ceilings and generally redesigned the old place. One of the results of his efforts was that a landing on the back stairs ended up going nowhere, blocked by the end wall of the new salon. At some point a small window was opened from this landing. Concealed from the salon by a moulding, it offered a clear, if distant, view from just below ceiling level of the whole room. Very few social events of any importance passed at Pemberton without an audience of servants viewing from this secret place. Usually they were too busy to do any more than take a few moments to glance and admire the dresses of the ladies or the dancing before hurrying back to the kitchens, but this evening a row of three chairs had been placed, and most of the staff from below stairs took their turn to listen to the famous soprano.

But Miss Hartley, the only staff member who knew opera and had followed the careers of both Alexander and Karlotta with passionate interest, did not join them.

CHAPTER 21

*I*n the housekeeper's pantry Eunice Parks, cup of tea in hand, lowered herself into her favourite armchair and with the sigh of someone who had been on her feet for many hours, lifted her worn but well-polished boots onto the padded fender. Closing her eyes, she allowed the glow of the fire to play over her face. The kitchens were near enough to hear the bustle of preparations, and the smell of roasting meats made its way across the flagstoned servants' corridor, but none of that was her concern.

A houseful of guests, most of them foreigners who didn't speak the language and had all manner of strange and unexpected requirements (the German doctor wanted his mattress moved to the floor!), had been installed in spring cleaned and newly-aired rooms. Bags had been unpacked, clothes hung, refreshed, ironed and returned. None of the housemaids had dropped or broken anything and none of the footmen had left a valise in the wrong room; in short the long-planned grand event was smoothly under way. This moment, as the company listened to the concert, was one of the rare and treasured pauses in Mrs Parks' long, long day. Later there would be beds to be turned down, fires to be tended, demands for bedding, hotwater bottles, who knew what else, but now, for a few precious moments, the housekeeper's time was her own.

The gentle strains of a fine soprano filtered down the stone back stairs. A harp accompanied the angelic sound, just as in heaven, Eunice thought, though perhaps in heaven her feet wouldn't be so sore.

Her cup and saucer, pretty but unmatched, began to tilt. A log shifted on the fire. One melody gave way to another upstairs and Mrs Parks' head began to sink towards her left shoulder. But if she dozed, she did so with the long-time housekeeper's permanent alertness. She was awake and on her feet by the time the youngest footman got up his courage and knocked a second time.

'Very sorry to disturb you, Mrs Parks, only it's Miss Hartley,' he said, when she opened the door.

'NETTY SAYS there's noises coming from her room.'

Dear God, not now, Mrs Parks thought, straightening her lace collar, *not during the concert*.

'Go back to Mr Swain,' she told the boy. 'I shall see to Miss Hartley.'

The housekeeper hurried along the corridor to the back staircase. Irritation sharpened the tap of her boots on the worn flagstones. Miss Lah-de-dah Hartley, was up to her old nonsense, was she? The housekeeper's eyes, as always, scanned for dust, cobwebs, misplaced objects or stray candlewax as she passed. She straightened a bowl of roses on the landing, scarcely breaking her step.

The wretched woman had made a nuisance of herself for months, she thought, stopping to listen for passing guests - it did not do for a hurrying housekeeper to take an aristocratic lady or gentleman by surprise. A housekeeper should radiate calm at all times, she should tread lightly in the corridors of the great house. Ideally, she should be invisible. She should certainly never stomp, rush or lose her temper - the very idea!

Mrs Parks tried not to grit her teeth. She had predicted trouble. Miss Hartley had been leading up to something with her aches and pains, her medicines, and her special food. Mrs Parks had seen such things before. She had seen them even in governesses - a breed more prone than most to nervous attacks and fits of strange behaviour, and above all else to giving themselves airs and having fancy ideas - but why, if Miss Hartley was to create a drama, did the dratted woman have to choose such an occasion to do it?

Miss Hartley needed a proper talking to.

Down the long bedroom corridor bustled Mrs Parks, still alert for dust or imperfection, until she reached the discreet door in the panelling at the end that led up the back stairs to the nursery landing.

Here the Turkey rugs of the bedroom corridor gave way to bare boards and oilcloth, though the passage was well-lit and wallpapered to match the nursery rooms above. The stairs twisted, emerging near the children's bedrooms. The governess's room was a little further along, beyond the schoolroom and nursery kitchen. Mrs Parks listened at young Master William's bedroom door, but heard no sound.

Netty the nursery maid was at her mending in the nursery kitchen. She sprang to her feet, always nervous at the senior woman's approach. Mrs Parks was famously fierce and Netty, at fifteen, lived in fear of her sharp tongue.

'What's all this, Netty?'

'It's Miss Hartley, Mrs Parks, she was making a lot of noise. Master William was in the playroom and he was worried, poor lad. I told him it was nothing, but it was horrible.'

'What kind of noise?'

'We could hear banging and bumping. I thought she was moving the furniture about, but when I listened at the door I could hear her moaning and making sounds. She might be ill, Mrs Parks. I was too scared to go in. I called to her, but she didn't answer. I didn't want to worry Master William, you know what he's like. He gets nightmares as it is.'

'Did you send him somewhere else?'

'Yes, I told both the boys to play in the long corridor until bedtime.'

'You stay here. Send anyone who comes away. I shall look in on Miss Hartley myself.'

CHAPTER 22

*W*hen Miss Hartley did not answer a knock at her door, Mrs Parks pressed her ear to it and rapped more loudly. 'Miss Hartley? It's Mrs Parks, are you asleep?'

The housekeeper pressed her ear to the door, but heard nothing. A queasy feeling crept into her stomach. She wondered whether to call for help. Swain was always reliable in an emergency, but dinner preparations would be well under way. She pictured the long formal dining table shining with silver. Swain checking the place settings with his measure. He could not possibly come away.

Mrs Parks turned her pass key in the lock and pushed, but the door did not open. It moved a little, as if something were against it. She pushed again and the door yielded an inch or two. Whatever was against the door on the inside was soft, not a piece of furniture, for example. Pushing a third time, Mrs Parks looked down to see what was blocking her way and caught a glimpse of soft fabric near the foot of the door. There was a scalloped edging, as you would see on a petticoat. Mrs Parks allowed the door to close again and turned her back to it, gathering herself.

Her immediate thought was this: the wretched woman is drunk. She has fallen over behind the door. Cursing all intemperance, the housekeeper turned back to the door and threw her whole weight against it several times.

The governess was lying on her side. Her eyes were half closed and her mouth was open. It was particularly shocking to Mrs Parks to see that Miss Hartley, neat, prim Miss Hartley, had her clothes crushed in rumpled disarray and her hair wild and askew. Her skin was waxen. Her lips tinged blue. Her dress was rucked up, showing thin legs and rumpled drawers beneath wrinkled petticoats.

The housekeeper stood for a few moments looking down at the fallen woman and taking in the details of the room around her. The bed was tidily made. There were no empty glasses or signs of drinking. A single book had fallen to the floor and a chair near the door lay on its side.

A tinkling Mozart air drifted into the governess's room from downstairs and with it a murmur of laughter and the distant hum of the concert under way downstairs.

Steeling herself, Mrs Parks reached to touch the hand that lay nearest on the rug. It was chilled, but so was the room. There was no fire in the grate. Mrs Parks shivered. She could see her own breath before her in the dim room. With a grunt of effort she knelt and put her cheek to the blue lips. Was there movement in the chest? Did she feel a breath against her cheek? By now the sound of her own pounding heart and the utter confusion of her thoughts made it impossible to know.

Mrs Parks struggled back to her feet and stepping back, leaned against the wall, breathing hard. She studied the faded primroses on the wallpaper, running her fingers briefly along their intertwining stems. When she moved again her manner was purposeful.

She emerged from the governess's room a few minutes later. Locking the door behind her, she turned briskly, straightened her posture, smoothed her skirts, tucked her hair back into its bun, and walked back along the passage to the nursery kitchen.

'Netty, Miss Hartley is unwell. I have settled her in bed and I shall visit her again in a little while. You will have to take over her duties. Help Miss Mary-Ann to undress later. Sleep in the room opposite Master William's tonight. I shall send Jeannie to help you at bedtime. Is that understood?'

'Yes, Mrs Parks,' said Netty, bobbing a curtsey.

'And Netty, we do not want to disturb the children or spoil the party, so it would be best to say nothing about this. Do you understand?'

'Yes, Mrs Parks, but what if I hear her cry out again? Should I send for you?'

'Ring the bell. I will come myself,' the housekeeper said.

Netty thought this unusually kind.

CHAPTER 23

*I*t could never be confessed in polite company, but Vita's education had left her with a blank spot where music was concerned. She had been to concerts and sung in church, of course, but when her friends passed happy afternoons playing the piano, the flute or the violin, Vita could only watch in admiration, whilst often surreptitiously reading a book.

Knowing nothing about it made her, if anything, a better audience member, for she was easily impressed. Her sensitivity had not been blunted by overexposure. Where someone with detailed knowledge might listen critically and hear faults or misinterpretations, Vita was easily transported with delight. Her imagination conjured up stories to explain the music - *now he is galloping through the woods - now she is in a rage and running through the storm*. She was impressed, as the truly ignorant are, by all the wrong things. How amazing that Lotti can hold her breath for so long, how astonishing that she can remember the words. Dramatic German songs - often about long journeys which end badly - were not her favourite, but the operatic arias, so passionate, so heartfelt, brought tears to her eyes. And in all this she was far from alone.

When the performance was at an end an enormous armful of flowers was presented to Lotti by a beaming and proprietorial Signor Ricci. He had sprung from his chair roaring 'bravo!' and 'encore!' and urged two additional songs from the pair already.

As the cheering and applause finally faded, Alexander stepped forward. He gestured for silence and took Lotti's hand in his, bringing it to his lips. 'Ladies and gentlemen,' he said. 'Thank you. And to add to our festivities this evening, I am delighted to announce that Miss Von Diepentahl has done me the great honour of accepting my proposal. Karlotta and I are engaged to be married!'

This, of course, brought a surge of applause and enthusiasm from the audience. The German aunts on either side beamed and tapped their folded fans. Vita looked across and saw Lady Pemberton smile in gracious acknowledgement of the news. Lord Pemberton, in his chair, nodded before Billings wheeled him away.

A gong sounded above the hubbub and Swain announced dinner. As the guests, in high spirits, began to move towards the dining room, Vita saw Signor Ricci dart towards Karlotta. Smiling and nodding most charmingly, he blocked her way. Alexander's hand was being shaken by almost every man in the room. He was swept into the crowd. His fiancée, though, was gently detained by the Italian.

Leaving the salon with the German aunts, Vita noticed how serious Karlotta's expression had suddenly become.

'Such delicious smells!' Gabrielle remarked. 'Wonderful music always brings a good appetite. Does it not?'

Beneath the chandeliers of the long parlour footmen were

weaving between the guests serving glasses of champagne. A string quartet struck up, the harpist filling the air with silvery ribbons of plucked harmony. The German aunts were drawn immediately into one excited group after another, congratulated and praised on all sides for their niece's talents, and the happy announcement of the engagement. Vita, observing from a corner, noticed that the sea of colourful noise and movement was hazier than usual, and realized she must have left her spectacles in the salon. She slipped back across the hall to find them.

Faced with ranks of empty chairs, it took Vita a few moments to locate the place she had occupied. Even then she could only peer around, suffering the usual irritating difficulty of needing glasses to find lost glasses. She was on the floor behind a sofa, feeling about, when she heard Lotti and Signor Ricci approach. Their conversation was hushed and intense.

'Alas, Miss Diepentahl, my sopranos are always single ladies. It is an iron rule with me. Marriage must wait until the world has taken a newcomer to its heart. People have to fall in love a little. You understand?'

'Alexander and I have yet to set a date, Signor Ricci,' Lotti said, as they passed. 'A long engagement would be perfectly possible.' Her tone was sweetly persuasive.

'Alas, even knowing a singer is engaged to be married is too much of a disadvantage.'

'I did not know this.'

'How could you? I only wish it were not so. Don't look sad. The world of the great performer is a harsh one. Many sacrifices are called for. You have made your choice. I adore your voice – I believe, as I said, that I could have taken you to the very heights, but you know your own heart.'

'You will dine with us, Signor Ricci, surely?'

'Alas, no. I am expected in London tonight.'

Vita's hand fell, at last, onto her lost spectacles and she stood up just as Lotti and Signor Ricci passed the door of the salon and the rest of their talk was lost in the music beyond.

CHAPTER 24

*C*ook always thought that from downstairs in the kitchens a large dinner party sounded like the rumble of a long storm. She rarely left the kitchens at such a time, as she was orchestrating the final stages of cooking. Monsieur, in his tall white hat, stationed near the stairs used by the servers, supervised the presentation of each finished dish. Under his scrutiny no dab of misplaced sauce, no wrongly-shaped carrot, mis-grilled fillet or under-seasoned soufflé could reach the dining room.

Although only the muted rumble of polite conversation, studded with an occasional crescendo of laughter, reached as far as the kitchens, chef and cook were both expert at interpreting the sounds of the dining room overhead. Conversation would begin quietly over the first two courses, but as the wine flowed and the company relaxed into the pleasures of the table - and these pleasures were considerable in this household - the volume of collected voices rose with each successive course. By the time desserts and fruit were being eaten, surges of laughter were louder and frequent enough to roll around overhead like summer thunder. These were the sounds the kitchen staff hoped for. They rated a dinner party a success when would-be speech makers had to tap their spoons on their crystal glasses insistently several times before they could call for silence and begin.

Their other source of information was the waiting staff. Swain and his footmen, who carried the food and attended the table, whilst hurrying to keep dishes warm, would deliver brief reports on how the food was being received above.

'Did they enjoy the poussin?' Cook would ask.

'Went down a treat,' Albert or Tom would reply, lifting the next laden salver from the table near the stairs.

'And his Lordship? Did he like the new sauce?'

'I saw him give Swain the nod.'

A nod from the master or mistress to Swain was the sign of highest approval. Seated at either end of the table, Lady Felicity in particular used a series of subtle signals to time the courses and indicate pleasure or displeasure. Waiting foot-men, standing to attention in their livery around the table watched carefully, trying to detect the code, but Swain kept the details to himself. Suffice to say that Swain at any moment knew precisely how the host and hostess wanted the dinner to proceed, whether it was satisfactory, whether more wine, or less, should be served, which guest might require more attention, which dishes were particularly enjoyed and when each course was over and the next should be brought in.

This dinner was rather late to begin. In the kitchens, chef and cook were anxiously delaying the moment of readiness for the first dishes, but they knew this was generally a good sign. It meant people were enjoying their conversation over the champagne in the salon, and Lady Felicity did not feel the need to hasten them through to the dining room.

By the time grace had been said (in *German*, Swain reported) and the company was seated and ready to begin, both chef and cook were eager to serve, so the soups - a mock turtle and the delicate consommé - were into the tureens and being ladled into dishes very rapidly.

'What if the Germans don't know the French words on the menu?' Mrs Dobbs wondered, 'how will they know which soup they want?'

'They know French too. All German people know French,' Alfred, the nearest footman said, 'the German lady told me.'

'Which German lady, Alfred? What are you doing talking to German ladies?'

'The famous one. The opera lady. Miss Von Whatsit. She came into the serving room just now. Very polite she was. She came to thank us for making her and her aunts welcome. She had a good look round. She said she liked the look of the soups.'

'Well I never,' said Mrs Dobbs.

'I imagine German people understand a French menu in the way that English people do - which is to say not very well,' Mr Picard remarked, once Alfred had left with a heavy tray. 'But these are educated people so perhaps they know more than most.'

'I should not like to eat a dinner without knowing what any of it was,' Cook said, straightening a prawn that was out of place on the layered pyramid display of seafood being prepared for the next course. 'At least with the seafood you can see what you're getting. Can't mistake an oyster for anything else, even if you are a foreigner, begging your pardon, Mr Picard.'

The dinner sounds from overhead were slightly different tonight, she thought, as she checked the ice in the buckets of oysters that had been brought in from the storeroom. The company seemed particularly merry - that would be the happy occasion of the engagement - but the collected voices were deeper than usual. German men had deeper voices than the usual English company, she concluded, uncertain whether this was a good or bad thing.

At first the seafood course went well. There was, a footman reported, a murmur of admiration round the table as the sumptuous displays of shellfish were brought to table. English diners, being brought up to believe it bad mannered to pay attention to food, never reacted in this way. The German guests had no such inhibitions and showed their delight by tucking napkins under their chins and setting energetically about the glistening oysters, lobster and prawns. Lady Felicity, who didn't much care for seafood herself, watched with approval as the beautifully constructed towers of shellfish were rapidly reduced to piles of shells, feelers, spidery legs and torn-off beady-eyed heads. Footmen rapidly swept them into silver buckets and bore them away.

CHAPTER 25

*P*reoccupied as she was with preparing duck and quail for the next course, Cook only gradually noticed a change in the sound from the dining room. An unexpected hush had fallen. A murmur of conversation followed, but its tone was different. As she moved to another hotplate and began stirring the sauce for the venison, she thought she heard a slight disturbance, perhaps a chair falling, and then many voices in tones that distinctly suggested alarm.

Monsieur, on the other side of the kitchen, was aligning an array of his delicate pastries on their stands, and caught her eye. Both stopped what they were doing and looked toward the kitchen stairs, expecting a footman to come down and tell them what had happened. Both at this point imagined a minor domestic difficulty: a spillage perhaps; something that might delay the other courses but cause no other harm.

No footman came.

Cook, increasingly aware of the unusual sounds coming from the dining room, looked about the kitchen and realised the three kitchen maids had all stopped what they were doing. They were looking at her in alarm.

'What's going on, Cook?' Annie, the scullery maid asked.

'Back to your work, Annie, please,' said Mrs Dobbs, 'Mr Swain will send George or Tom down in a minute.'

Monsieur Picard was closest to the kitchen stairs, but he had returned to the delicate placement of tarts and iced pastries on their stands.

'Shall I send Jeannie up to see if there is to be a delay, Mister Picard? I don't want these duck breasts over-cooked.'

'Yes, if her sauce will not burn,' said Monsieur.

Jeannie, the senior kitchen maid, a level-headed girl, removed her apron and dried her hands.

'Just look into the dining room from the serving room, Jeannie, and see if we need to delay the next course. Perhaps one of the ladies has fainted,' Mrs Dobbs suggested, as Jeannie hurried past.

Somewhere upstairs a door opened and for a few seconds the sound of the dining room washed over the landing and down into the kitchen at full volume. They heard shouts, running footsteps, urgent cries. By now nobody in the kitchen was concentrating on the food. As one they looked towards the stairs. A long moment passed, during which sauces steamed and duck breasts continued to hiss in the pan, and then with a clatter of boots Jeannie rushed back down to the kitchen. She was pale and breathless with the shock of what she had seen.

'They're sick, Mrs Dobbs. Lots of them. The young German lady has fallen down and they don't know if she's breathing. They were all crowded round. Swain says Annie should bring buckets. They've sent for Doctor Mills. One of the German men is a doctor too. It's terrible, Mrs Dobbs. They're all running about. The ladies are crying out for help and everyone is frantic.'

'And the master and mistress?'

'They were helping the young German lady. I think she might be dying, Mrs Dobbs.' Jeannie gasped for breath and pressed her hands to her face. Tears began to run between her fingers.

'We'll need to put the kettle on in case anyone wants tea,' Mrs Dobbs said and bustled to do it herself, comforted by a familiar activity among this sudden breakdown of normality.

'We shall suspend service, Mrs Dobbs. Do you agree?' said Monsieur Picard.

'I do agree. Shall we move what's ready to the hot cupboard upstairs in the serving room?'

'No, we must keep the other food away from the dining room,' said the chef. His face looked strange to Mrs Dobbs. His complexion was grey and even the way he stood made him seem suddenly older. He pulled his tall chef's toque from his head, and walked through the kitchens past the pantry and stores and out of the back door into the yard.

CHAPTER 26

*T*he German doctor among the guests that night, Herr Dr Julius Zecker, was a skin specialist. It had been many years since he had practiced any sort of medicine except the prescribing of coloured ointments and herbal baths. Before becoming personal physician to the Von Diepentahls, his practice had been in a spa town favoured by wealthy widows, who were inclined to adopt dear Dr Zecker and consult him long after their condition had healed.

Julius Zecker was a vegetarian and a natural aesthete. He believed in long walks in all weathers, did not touch alcohol or coffee and preferred to sleep - though his patients did not know this - on the floor at night. He had a passion for English country house architecture. A large part of the reason he accepted the invitation to this party was to see Pemberton Hall's Palladian exterior and rotunda for himself. He hoped to visit other country houses in the area. Combining his two great interests, buildings and medicine, he was developing a theory about the effect of different architectural styles on health. His early thesis was that bodily health was greatly strengthened and sustained by symmetry, though whether symmetry of straight line or curve was more effective, he had yet to ascertain.

Dr Zecker's first reaction, when the sickness set in around him, was fervently to wish himself elsewhere. However, his training soon asserted itself and by the time it was clear that the evening would not be proceeding as planned, he was directing servants to assist guests who had been taken ill, and helping Karlotta as best he could. Karlotta was the first and the most violently affected. She had risen suddenly from the table soon after the shellfish displays had been presented and, struggling to take a step or two toward the door, appeared to have fainted. The first reaction around the table had been mild concern only; a lady fainting was not, after all, so very rare, but Karlotta had then woken and almost immediately begun to vomit with such repeated violence that the doctor had hurried over and the whole table had stopped eating in horror.

Within moments two or three other guests had begun to retch and try to rise from their seats, but the violence of the onset of the sickness caused them to fall to the ground, help-less. Soon a third of the guests were indisposed, and the others were paralysed either by horror or by their own nausea. Swain and his footmen ran from one group to the next, but could do little more than proffer cushions, bowls or cloths. Those who had collapsed around the table were too weak to be moved at first. Under the directions of the German doctor they were lifted and propped around the walls, the clothing around their necks was loosened, and their faces were bathed with cooling water between bouts of sickness.

Those who were not affected he ordered out of the dining room, directing them to retire to their own rooms and stay there. If they felt unwell they were to call for assistance, but not to mix with other guests. Although every early indication suggested poisoning, Doctor Zecker could not rule out a contagion of some sort this early. In case this was an infection, he wanted as many guests as possible isolated. Besides, it lessened the pandemonium in the dining room.

VITA HAD WATCHED in alarm as the scene unfolded. She had been preoccupied, when the shellfish first appeared, with Lotti's two aunts. Over the soup they had begun discussing gardening, a topic for which Vita had prepared one or two conversational starters such as: 'Do you favour the formal style of garden, or the more informal?' but very little progress had been made because both old ladies were enthusiastic about their dinner and wanted the menu translated. This ought to have been straightforward, but Vita had not allowed for the complication of Mock Turtle Soup, which took a lot of explaining. Both aunts eventually liked the sound of it, and were relieved that no turtles were involved.

'The chicken looks very weak to me. I prefer a strong soup,' Tante Gabrielle remarked, 'Vita, you should choose it too. She will have this one, also' she directed the footman.

The aunts, perhaps because of their long experience in life, seemed less shaken by the sudden onset of sickness all around them than many of the other guests. For practical reasons - from their seats even the nearest shellfish pyramid was out of reach - they had not been quick to begin the next course. Lotti collapsed almost as soon as the footman had served the old ladies, and this was such a distraction that neither had touched oysters or crayfish, so both were soon guided safely to their bedrooms. Once they were settled, Vita came back to see what she could do to help downstairs.

CHAPTER 27

*D*octor Mills arrived within an hour of Lotti's collapse. Mills was the local man who had tended to the Pemberton family for years. Some thought him a little old-fashioned but such doubts were as nothing at a time like this. As the German guests clung to Herr Doktor Zecker, so the English hosts felt better the moment Albert Mills's worn riding boots clumped up the broad curve of the stairs. Lady Pemberton introduced the two medical men in the dining room and watched warily, as one would watch two dogs meeting in a park. With Vita translating, Dr Zecker explained the onset of the illness and what he had done so far; Mills listened and in general seemed to agree. The two doctors moved from patient to patient, taking pulses and feeling foreheads for fever. Mills, a portly man, found bending down to patients on the floor very inconvenient, so left that to his younger colleague.

The dining room was a little calmer now. One by one the guests recovered sufficiently to be helped first onto chairs, and then to their rooms. Vita walked two or three of them back, helped by a maid or footman, and assisted the guests to their own beds, where the doctors visited, making rounds, as if in a particularly comfortable hospital. By midnight most patients were either sleeping peacefully or sipping camomile tea and feeling a little better.

Through the night the doctors continued their visits, but by dawn it was clear that only Karlotta's condition remained serious. She had been carried by two willing footmen to her room, and remained feverish, drifting in and out of consciousness throughout the night. Both her aunts stayed at her bedside, bathing her forehead and speaking to her gently by turns. Alexander tried to visit several times, but was only allowed to glance at the patient from the door, the aunts convinced that all stimulation was to be avoided. He paced the corridor outside the room at first, later dozing occasionally on a chair. By morning he had still not changed out of his dress suit from the night before, but the stiff shirt front was buckled and one side of the collar had come adrift. His hair stood out from his head and the pallor of his face and dark circles under his eyes made him look alarming enough for Swain to lead him firmly back to his room for at least a change of clothing.

Mills spent the night at Pemberton Hall, and both doctors were back with their patients for an early round soon after seven. They were accompanied by Vita, who was already indispensable to both doctors. At the height of the outbreak, it was Vita who kept a sheet of notes on each patient, carried them boiled water to drink, soothed them by bathing their faces and hands, noted their temperature. Apart from that she saw when the doctors were tired, sending for food and drink to sustain them, specifying vegetarian food and herbal tea for Dr Zecker.

The two anxious aunts were persuaded from Lotti's

bedside to take a little rest and sustenance themselves only with a promise that Vita and Dr Zecker would take their places and send for them the moment there was any change in the patient's condition. By eight, Zecker found that Lotti's fever had begun to decline. She seemed calmer and fell into a normal sleep.

'I shall go and tell her aunts,' Zecker told her. 'I gave them my solemn word I would do so, and they will be cheered by this improvement.'

'Yes, by all means,' Vita said. 'I shall wait here.'

'There would be no harm in sleeping a little in the chair, Miss Carew, there seems to be no danger of a sudden change now, and we medical people must learn to sleep whenever the chance arises, I think.'

Vita, felt pleased to be included in the category of 'medical people'. She stayed at the bedside, but did allow herself to sit back in her chair and relax for the first time in many hours. Her eyes were almost closed when she registered a change in the patient. Lotti blinked and looked around.

'Is nobody there?' she asked, quietly.

Vita realised that the chair she was sitting in was out of the patient's sight , hidden by the draperies around the bed. She was about to answer, when Lotti continued speaking drowsily, apparently to herself.

'Bravo Lotti!' the young woman in the bed said. 'A fine performance. One of your best. But so tiring! She yawned and stretched. 'And obviously one has to miss breakfast, which is a great shame.'

Was Lotti delirious? She did not seem delirious. She seemed conscious. Vita wondered what she should do.

Alexander put his head around the door and called in a stage whisper, 'Miss Carew, may I come in?'

He was already inside the room, stepping anxiously

toward the bed, but stopped half way, seeming unable to bring himself to approach any further.

'How is she?'

'She seems a little better now,' Vita said, still not certain of what she had heard.

'May I approach?'

'Yes, there is nothing to worry about.'

Alexander came to the other side of the bed and looked searchingly at the lovely young woman - for Karlotta was beautiful even in sickness - her hair a loose mass of soft honey-brown strands twisting about the pillow and around her face. She now appeared deeply asleep.

'Oh, Lotti. My poor Lotti,' he said, 'I am so sorry. Please forgive me.'

The patient slept on, her breathing calm and steady.

'This is my fault,' Alexander said to Vita. 'It was I who urged Mama to serve shellfish. It is all my doing. Lotti told me that she loved shellfish and oysters in particular. She had only tried them once, in Paris, and she had adored them. I took it into my head to put them on the menu for this dinner. It was a last minute decision. I had to persuade Mama because of the cost, but she agreed and set Monsieur Picard to find oysters at two days' notice. Which he did. All to please Lotti. It was a foolish whim. I see that now. I hold myself entirely responsible for this dreadful accident and to think that it nearly killed dear Lotti. I can hardly bear the thought.'

Vita did not know what to say to this. The logic was faulty, but she could tell that logical argument alone would not make Alexander feel better. 'She is far stronger now,' she told him.

But he was not to be comforted. 'She may never forgive me,' he said. 'I fear I have destroyed her health and our happiness. Oh Lotti! What have I done?' Alexander whispered, and left the room without another word.

CHAPTER 28

*F*or several moments all that could be heard was the peaceful breathing of the patient, and bird-song outside the window. The curtains were closed and Vita was considering opening them a little when footsteps in the corridor warned her of a hastening approach. Swain the butler opened the door. He stepped inside and held it behind him.

'Miss Carew, the German doctor would like you to come and speak for him. There has been...'

Here his words failed him, but his expression alone was enough to tell Vita something dreadful was amiss.

'I have asked a maid to sit with Miss Diepentahl until her aunts return, she will be here soon. Please come immediately. I will meet you at the main stairs.'

As soon as the maid arrived, Vita hurried along the corridor. Swain was at the staircase and wordlessly led her up to the nursery rooms. There he suddenly stopped short. 'To warn you, Miss Carew, there has been a discovery.'

Vita could not help looking around the butler towards the open doorway. It was Miss Hartley's room. She could hear the voices of both doctors. She looked at Swain in alarm.

'Is it Miss Hartley?' she asked.

'It is, Miss. I'm afraid she was found this morning.'

'Found? You mean she is ill?'

'I'm afraid she has been found dead, Miss. I regret to tell you so suddenly, but the doctors asked that you be called. They want someone to write their observations down for them. I did offer to do this myself, but they said you were used to them and you have the language. I hope this is not too upsetting.'

'Miss Hartley is dead? I can hardly believe it,' Vita said, but she followed Swain to the open door of the governess's room.

The doctors both turned and looked at Vita. They had been bent over a figure on the bed. Even from the door Vita could see the figure was lifeless. It was distressing to see the expression on the face of the dead woman, who appeared anguished. Her mouth was open and her lips pulled back in an ugly grin. The teeth, Vita could not help but see, were very poor. Some brown and others darker, particularly towards the back. Several were missing.

'Miss Carew. You have helped us very efficiently so far. Would you be willing and able to continue now, as we examine this poor woman? I am keen to begin and Dr Zecker and I are agreed that someone needs to take notes. Of course, I shall perfectly understand if ...' Mills was saying, but Vita interrupted.

'... I am willing to assist, I only need to find paper and a pen.' She looked around, but none was obvious in the Governess's bare room.

'The schoolroom. There will be some in the schoolroom.' This was Mrs Parks, from a corner of the room. The housekeeper crossed the corridor and quickly returned with an empty exercise book and a pencil. Her hands shook as she gave them to Vita and backed away. 'If I am no longer needed here, I shall leave you for now,' she muttered, and they heard her hastening footsteps down the corridor.

'She was very shocked,' Zecker said. 'It was she who found her. I was in my room and heard her scream ...'

'I will begin a thorough examination with a view to establishing the cause of death,' Mills said, interrupting. If you could just make notes of what I say, Miss Carew. Agreed?'

Vita translated and the German doctor agreed.

'May I ask why she is so rigid? It is not usual is it?' Vita said to Mills, as he hung his tweed jacket on the back of a chair and began rolling up his shirt sleeves. The doctor shrugged.

'*Rigor mortis*. It depends on several factors. We don't know enough to say, yet. Now write this down, please: the patient was found by the housekeeper at ...' He hesitated and looked at Dr Zecker.

'Can you remember the exact time, Dr Zecker?'

Vita translated.

'Eight ten, approximately,' Zecker replied. 'We were called at eight seventeen. I looked at my watch.'

Vita gave his answer in English and wrote it down.

'Yes. The patient was found by the housekeeper at eight ten and Dr Zecker arrived a few moments before I did. Both of us took her pulse and carried out the other usual tests for morbidity and pronounced the patient dead at half past eight. I heard the clock strike.'

'Should we make a note of where she was found?' Vita asked.

'Yes. We found the patient on the floor between her bed and the door. There appeared to have been a good deal of movement in the throes of death. That is to say she seemed to have moved around the room. Several items were in disarray and her clothing was caught around her.'

Vita wrote the troubling details down as calmly as she could and translated what Mills had said to Dr Zecker, who nodded.

'There were no signs of injury immediately evident. There was some discolouration to the skin, which seemed yellow, and the lips were blue.'

'I observed a yellowish powder deposited on her lips,' Zecker put in, once he had heard the translation. 'I should like that recorded.'

'I made no such observation,' Mills said, but he did not object to the German doctor's addition.

'We both noticed that the body was in a state of rigor mortis which seemed to have set in some hours before. We shall now need to remove the deceased woman's clothing, Miss Carew. It may not be easy to do so. We may need to cut it.'

*I*f Vita had felt sorry for Miss Hartley before, she certainly felt great pity for her now. Her dress and underclothes were cut away to reveal a grey gaunt body, still clenched in rigor, as angular and pale as a skeleton carved on a marble tomb. Her hair, bunched and sticky, almost covered her face, but not completely enough to hide the disturbing silent shriek she ended her life giving. Dr Mills, without mentioning it, leaned over and applied enough pressure to close her eyelids.

'The body is thin. She is considerably underweight. There are old scars but no recent injuries that I can see. Apart from this, the only abnormality is a light swelling to the left lower jaw. Do you see that, Zecker?'

The German doctor, once the question was understood, examined the jaw himself. 'Yes,' he said, 'a dental abscess, I would guess.'

Mills nodded. 'When we can open the mouth again, we will establish the cause, but for now, we will just note the presence of the swelling.'

Vita did so. The doctors together rolled the body over, but

there were no abnormalities to be seen on the woman's back, except that it was thin enough for the bones to show clearly under the skin.

'My conclusion, at this early stage, would be that the cause of death was medical. It is unlikely to be food poisoning associated with the cases we attended yesterday. What do you think, Zecker?'

The German doctor looked at the body in his turn. He examined the fingernails and toes as well as feeling the neck and head. 'I can add little to Dr Mills' conclusions,' he said 'I would not want to eliminate other causes of death, such as a crisis of the heart or a brain seizure entirely, but it does not look like poisoning to me. It is unusual for rigor to set in so rapidly.'

Vita wrote all this into the notes. There was a pause as the doctors covered the body again and did what they could to restore some dignity to the governess by pulling the bedcovers awkwardly over her corpse.

'If I might make a suggestion, it would be helpful, perhaps, to write into the notes a few observations about the room itself,' Dr Zecker told them. 'I have once before been involved in a police investigation, and they were particularly concerned with this sort of circumstantial detail. No doubt the housekeeper will soon want to set the room to rights, so the moment to make such notes would be now, immediately.'

'Why does he talk of the police?' Mills asked, when Vita finished translating. 'I see no need to involve the police whatsoever.' He was rolling down his shirt sleeves.

Zecker began a tour of the room, speaking his observations aloud so that Vita could note them down. 'A rapid survey of the room shows that a small side table, a chair and a bookshelf have been overturned. There are several books on the floor. The bed is disordered, and the covers are twisted on the floor. The patient had perhaps been entangled in the sheets and dragged them from the bed behind her in a struggle to reach the door.' Zecker walked over to the door and bent to study it closely.

'What is he saying?' Mills put in. 'He seems to be speaking at length. Does this concern me?'

'He is simply recording the condition of the room, the bed and so on,' Vita explained.

Mills seemed uninterested in this. Zecker continued, 'On her nightstand is an empty glass, which has a trace of liquid left in it. We should keep this, it may tell us that she drank something before she died, some medicine or sleeping draft. Ask Doctor Mills, if you would be so kind, whether he himself prescribed any medicines to this governess.'

Vita did this. Mills, now shrugging his jacket back on, said no at first, then added, 'I did last year prescribe a tonic but nothing since.'

'A tonic? As treatment for what ailment?' Zecker asked, when he heard this.

Vita translated.

'Some digestive ailment, I'd have to consult my records to be certain. Miss Hartley was, in general, someone who suffered regular poor health and many minor ailments.'

Doctor Zecker continued moving about the room, he looked into a writing desk and slid open the small top drawer in a chest of drawers.

'I must say I do not see the point of this prying,' Mills remarked. He told Vita to translate this.

Zecker closed the drawer and gave a slight bow of acknowledgement to the senior doctor.

'Well, we need not detain you further, Miss Carew. As long as your notes are clear, you have been of important assistance to us, and in a way, to the unfortunate Miss Hartley as well,' Dr Mills told Vita. 'Leave your notes on the table over there, and I shall take charge of them. I shall need to discuss this situation with Lord and Lady Pemberton immediately, as I'm sure you will understand.'

Dr Zecker went over to the bowl of water provided by the bedside and washed his hands. Vita was about to do as Mills asked and leave her notes, but the German doctor looked up and caught her eye. He looked sharply towards the notes in her hand. Without a change of expression his look conveyed some hint that Vita registered.

'I have written very hasty notes, gentlemen. If you have finished this first examination, I should like to go and make a fair copy of them before I hand them over. I shall bring you the notes very soon.'

With that, Vita hurried out of the room, holding the papers close to her chest.

IN THE CORRIDOR Vita found Mrs Parks leaning, as if exhausted against a wall. She looked as if she had been weeping.

'Have the doctors finished? What did they say?' she asked.

'They only carried out a general inspection of Miss Hartley's body,' Vita told her.

'And do they know how she died?'

'Not yet.'

'Poisoning?'

'What makes you think that?'

'She'd likely had some of the shellfish. She often asked for dinner in her room.'

The housekeeper was agitated, which Vita thought only natural.

'I'm sorry, but the doctors do not know. They could not tell. That is one of several possibilities that were mentioned.'

'I expect they will have to call the police, or the coroner.' Mrs Parks was turning a handkerchief over in her hands. She seemed unable to take her eyes from the door of the governess's room. Her face was blotched and puffy. 'I must make arrangements for her to be laid out. The funeral ...'

'Her family?' Vita suggested.

'She has none. She is an orphan and an only child. Alone in the world, she always said.'

Vita had no answer to this, nor did she quite know what the procedure ought to be in a great house when a member of staff died suddenly. She was at a loss.

'Oh dear, and the children,' the housekeeper suddenly said, 'nobody has told them. They were fond of her. I must speak to their mother immediately.' Stimulated to action by the thought, she hurried away.

CHAPTER 30

*V*ita took her notes to the library as a place that offered a little seclusion, and began to re-write them at her usual little table. She had not been there long before Dr Zecker came in. He did not sit, but stood awkwardly some distance from where she was writing.

'Thank you for writing the notes,' he said.

'I was glad to be of help.'

'Miss Carew, did you observe anything unusual in the room of the unfortunate governess? I ask this because I am a foreigner and you are more familiar with the rooms of an English family and their servants.'

'I saw only an extremely bare room, nothing unusual, I don't think.'

'It was unusually bare, that is true. I have seen more possessions in a nun's cell than Miss Hartley seemed to own.'

'There were a number of books.'

'No cosmetics; no ladies' things.'

'Perhaps they were in her trunk or a drawer.'

'I looked - only briefly - but there was no sign.'

'It was an austere room, I agree, but perhaps she was that sort of person.'

'No pictures, no flowers in vases, not even the smallest amount of jewellery.'

'She wore earrings.'

'One single pair. She had no others. And no finery, no shawls, scarves or pretty hats. She had nothing. Almost nothing. Is this usual? In a great house like this a member of the household lives as poorly as that? She cannot even afford a brooch or a vase for a few flowers? I am shocked, by this Miss Carew, truly.'

He looked over his shoulder. 'I do not want to be seen talking to you. It would suggest a conspiracy to Dr Mills, and the German ladies would not approve, even if it is in the nature of a professional discussion. I will go now. Please, when you have written out your fair copy, make sure that nobody, not Dr Mills or anyone else, is given both copies of your notes. Keep one yourself.'

'A professional discussion' he had called it. Vita, though not entirely sure what he had meant, felt quietly pleased. As she wrote she wondered about what he had said. Miss Hartley's room was certainly bare. She wondered whether there was anyone she could ask about this. At this moment little William Pemberton came into the library.

'Hello,' he said. 'Are you doing your lessons here? I do mine in the schoolroom upstairs. That is a lot of writing.' The boy was glancing at the sheets of paper Vita had on the table before her. He looked at her with sympathy. 'I had to write two pages once. It took all morning on Wednesday and half of Thursday morning too.'

Vita quickly piled the pages together, alarmed at the thought that little William might be able to read the contents.

'Mama would like to see you in her sitting room,' William added. 'I will show you the way.'

~

LADY FELICITY RAN her hand over her eyes and motioned for Vita to sit in the chair beside her.

'I wanted to thank you, Vita, for your assistance during these terrible events.'

'Are the German guests leaving?' Vita asked. The window overlooked the drive and they could see three carriages now, all having trunks and hatboxes loaded onto them.

Felicity Pemberton sighed. 'All but Karlotta and her aunts. She is not well enough to travel yet, so they will stay with her a little longer. They have sent for a German cook from London to prepare their meals while they are here. I have had to banish Monsieur Picard from his own kitchen. He is outraged. The staff are up in arms.'

'Karlotta is much stronger this morning,' Vita said, hoping to change the subject to something more cheering.

'Yes, Mills said she was a little better. That is one mercy. I believe you went with the doctors to Miss Hartley's room, Vita.'

'Yes. They asked for a translator and I took notes for them as they carried out the examination.'

'Did they come to a conclusion?'

'Not yet. They did not find any obvious cause of death. She did not appear to have suffered an apoplexy or fit of any kind, but there can be no certainty at this stage.'

'It could be poisoning, then?'

'They have not come to a conclusion yet. She was not at the dinner, so ...'

'She often took food from the kitchens and carried it to her rooms, she could easily have done so last night.'

'There were no signs that suggested that. No plates or cutlery. The doctors were struck, in general, by how bare the room was. She seemed to have lived a very austere life.'

Lady Pemberton looked puzzled. 'Austere? Her rooms are comfortable, surely? My children are often there with her. They have never said anything. She never asked for anything, that I know of.'

Vita did not want to add to her hostess's anguish, saying only, 'She seemed to have few personal possessions. No little valuables, no jewellery or ornaments.'

'She had one or two cameo brooches, I remember seeing them, and some rather pretty amber earrings.'

'There was nothing like that in her room.'

Lady Pemberton seemed to dismiss that train of thought. 'Vita, you must be exhausted. Cook will send some breakfast up to the Yellow Room and you can, perhaps, get a little rest.'

'What will you tell the children? Perhaps it is not my concern, but William knows something is amiss.'

'His father and I have decided to tell both children when they come back from their ride. We shall say that Miss Hartley has very sadly died, but no more. We will not offer any explanation. I have already forbidden the staff from speculating about the matter. Above all they must not do so in front of the children.'

'William and Mary-Anne must have been fond of her,' Vita said.

Lady Pemberton paused briefly, frowning, but then said, 'They have known her all their lives, they have probably eaten more meals with Miss Hartley than they have with their father and I ...'

She broke off, looking away briefly, but when she

resumed her manner was business-like again. 'Now I must occupy myself with the remaining guests and Alexander. The dear boy is beside himself with anxiety. He has not slept and refuses to eat. Karlotta will not see him. Or perhaps it is her aunts who do not allow him into her room, I don't know.'

Vita made to leave, but Lady Pemberton took her sleeve, speaking urgently. 'Vita, does either of the doctors speak of involving the police?'

'The police? They have not said …'

'If they do. I would be most grateful if you could … you see one would want to avoid … to avoid … any damage to the reputation of the family, of Pemberton, it would be disastrous. And surely there is nothing to be gained?'

'The police have not been mentioned so far,' Vita told her.

'I shall speak to Mills, of course, he is always very obliging, but the German doctor - who knows what ideas he may have? You will let me know if you hear any mention of the police, Vita?'

'Certainly,' Vita said, but left feeling uncomfortable with her own promise.

CHAPTER 31

$\mathcal{V}$ita met Swain in the corridor as she left Lady Pemberton. The butler looked as elegant as usual, but there were dark shadows under his eyes.

'If you would care for some breakfast, Miss? Shall I send a maid to the Yellow Room with a tray?'

'Thank you. Perhaps some tea,' Vita said, gratefully. She made her way up the staircase where, in the painting, the white monkey still howled silently and the cockerel's eyes still rolled in its severed head.

The Yellow Room was no warmer or more welcoming, but tea and toast soon arrived on a tray. Did she imagine it, or were the servants being particularly kind to her this morning? She took a little tea and was almost immediately overcome with exhaustion, falling onto the huge bed and sleeping so soundly that when she awoke it took several minutes to remember where she was and then, with a shudder, recall the drama of the long day and night before.

It was nearly noon. A soft rain was falling outside. Some-where nearby a song thrush sang. Vita felt a sudden longing for fresh air, but first a wash and a change of clothes. She had attended the sick all night and then fallen asleep in Miss Pushkin's lovely blue evening gown. What a shame, Vita thought, looking in the mirror, that even if it could be properly cleaned, she would never be able to wear it again without instantly being reminded of the sights, sounds and smells of its first outing.

At the washstand, as she washed her face and hands and brushed her hair, Vita became aware of voices. The sounds were coming from an odd direction. Pulling on her day dress, she walked across to the fireplaces on the opposite wall. The noise was louder near the blocked off fireplace. Leaning in, Vita could see a sacking bundle had been used to block the chimney's draft. She pulled, and it slumped into the empty fireplace, followed by a cloudy gust of dust and soot. The voices were clearer. The first was the housekeeper.

'Netty, what will you tell them? If they ask.'

A wordless sound came in reply, something like a sob or a gasp.

'Tell me what you said before, girl. I won't be annoyed.'

'Miss Hartley went to her rooms…'

'When? When? The time is important, girl. When did she go?'

'After…after the music started…'

'…Not after, *when*. *When* the music started.'

The younger voice was high-pitched with fear. 'I might get it wrong, Mrs Parks. I might say the wrong thing.'

'You saw Miss Hartley go to her rooms when the music started. You saw nothing and heard nothing else.'

'But Mrs Parks…I did. I heard noises. That's why I rang.'

'You thought you did, Netty, but you were wrong. There were no noises.'

'But…'

'There were no noises. No noises. Understood? There could be trouble, Netty, if you get this wrong.'

'Yes, Mrs Parks.'

'You're sure now?'

'Yes, Mrs Parks.'

'Now, dry your eyes. It's not so difficult, is it?'

'No, Mrs Parks.'

The girl sounded terrified.

WHEN, downstairs, one of the maids brought her raincoat, Vita asked if there was a younger maid called Netty.

'Yes, Miss. Netty Harris. She helps in the nursery,' she replied.

'I'd like a breath of air in the garden, which is the nearest door?'

'The quickest way is along here, if you don't mind using the servants' corridor,' said the maid. 'Shall I show you?'

'No, thank you, I can see the way,' Vita told her, and made her way along the long underground passageway to the small back door.

On this side of the house there were formal gardens with sculpted yews and gravel paths. Vita followed the path which curved between hedges to an elaborately wrought high gate. She would have loved to stroll over the park and up as far as the folly, but the rain was already coming through her coat onto her shoulders, so she turned back, following another path into the woodland garden surrounding what she soon realised was an orangery. There was nobody around, so she sat on a stone bench under the arched porch to take cover from the rain, listening to a song thrush in a tall beech and breathing with pleasure the rain-scented air.

CHAPTER 32

a figure, a man in a raincoat wearing a large Homburg hat and carrying an umbrella, came along the path towards her. She could not see who it was and wondered whether she should identify herself, but this proved unnecessary as he made straight for her, bowing as he reached the bench.

'Mademoiselle,' he said, 'I wonder if I may trouble you for a moment of your time?'

Vita did not object. The man stepped under the portico out of the rain, folded his umbrella and removed his hat.

'I am Emile Picard,' he said, 'I am the chef here at Pemberton Hall.'

Vita hardly knew what to say. Here was someone else whose night had been a catastrophe. She held out her hand to the chef and he, surprised, took it gratefully and shook it. 'My name is Vita Carew, I am a guest. I came with my Aunt, Mrs Brocklehurst.'

'And you made the translation for the doctors during the night, I heard.'

'I did.'

'You also helped them when they found the poor Miss Hartley this morning.'

'Yes. Sadly.'

The chef stood holding his hat in both hands. He looked down and turned it slowly, seeming to search for the words he needed. 'Miss Carew, I did not cause the poisoning last night. No food that was unfit came from my kitchen, I am certain of it.'

'Why do you tell me this?' Vita asked him.

The chef continued to rotate his hat. He did not look up, but even the top of his bowed head communicated misery. 'Nobody has spoken to me. Nobody has asked my opinion. You at least, as a guest, someone who is an outsider, might listen to what I say. The doctors trust you. They might listen.'

'I have no special influence as far as the doctors are concerned. It may be the police you need to speak to.'

'Ah! The police!' he exclaimed, in despairing tones. 'It has come to this! Defending my kitchen to the police!'

'I'm sure if you just tell them what happened ...'

But the chef was now trembling so much that he dropped his hat and it fell among the dried leaves on the tiled floor. 'Mademoiselle,' he said, 'do you imagine that the word of a chef will carry any weight against that of the noble ladies and gentlemen who were taken ill last night? It will make no difference what I say, I am the one who will be blamed. It seems there is nothing I can do to defend myself and my kitchen. The shellfish was good. It was fresh, it was well-stored, there was nothing wrong with it. Do you think I could grow up in Brittany, near the sea, and work as a chef all my life without knowing good seafood when I see it? It was superb, the shellfish we served last night. The best, the highest quality. I tasted it myself, I examined everything. It did not cause the sickness!'

'Then you must simply tell them.'

He picked the hat off the ground and began brushing leaves from its soft pile. His hair and moustache were white and he had the cleanest and most perfectly manicured fingernails Vita had ever noticed.

'Will you speak for me, Mademoiselle? You know French, I think.'

'But Monsieur Picard, your English is perfect.'

'Please. I have nobody else to ask. I may not know the exact English words I need. I stand to lose …' he made an open-handed gesture of despair, 'everything.'

The chef looked directly up at her for the first time. His eyes were a striking blue and glistened with tears.

'Of course,' she said, 'I will do what little I can.'

The chef replaced his hat and stood to attention. 'I am most grateful to you, Mademoiselle Carew. And now I will leave you in peace to your contemplations.'

'Before you go, Monsieur Picard,' Vita said, remembering, 'yesterday I saw Miss Hartley enter a room in the basement. It said *Chef* on the door.'

Picard looked up sharply. 'Yes, she had taken to visiting my room. She was there at yesterday. She took my reading glasses and left a letter,' he said.

Vita looked at the chef steadily. 'She took your reading glasses?'

'She was in the habit of taking small things. Not just from me, but from others too. Lately she had removed several small items of mine.'

'Why did she do that?'

'A form of madness, I think. Perhaps she needed money, but I think it was only a sort of habit. Also she wanted a reason to speak to me. If she took something, she could return it. It would be an excuse to start a conversation.'

'Was she so lonely that she had to do that?'

'Miss Carew. You are young. Too young to understand, I imagine. Miss Hartley had deceived herself into believing I favoured her company. It was not so. I once spoke with her, but briefly, about opera. I know a little of the opera. I am fond of its music. In Paris I visited the opera and saw some of the great stars.'

The chef smiled wryly, as he remembered happier times.

'I mentioned this. It was one single conversation, but it was enough to make Miss Hartley believe we had enough in common to ...' He struggled for words.

Vita waited, shivering a little and pulling her coat around her for warmth.

'... to become close friends. She began to visit my room. Come into the kitchens. Write me notes. She had misunderstood. I wanted no such thing. I did not encourage her. She began to write the most ... the most *exaggerated* letters several times a day. I have a large collection. Even the most blunt repudiation had no effect. I begged her to stop, but anything I said or did was interpreted as encouragement.'

The chef shook his head.

'Does her letter help to explain what happened?'

'You can see for yourself, Miss Carew,' he said and handed Vita a small envelope he took from his pocket. The rain had made it damp.

Vita read:

My Dear Emile,

I beg you to allow me one last note.

I hope you enjoy Alexander's performance tonight. It will be wonderful, I know. I long to hear it myself, but I shall not. I am unwell and my presence is unwanted.

Unwanted - the word attaches itself to me like a leech!

Do not concern yourself, my dear Emile, I shall trouble

you no longer. I have a strong sleeping draught. It will grant me the peace I so often lack and help to put behind me the agonising series of snubs and slights that are my daily reward for fifteen years of service to this family.

Your most sincere friend,

Ada Hartley.

'Did you read this as a permanent farewell, Monsieur Picard?' Vita asked.

'Permanent? No! I read it as her reason for missing the concert. Her health has been poor, she takes medicine - a lot of medicine for pain.'

'This is the sleeping draught she refers to?'

'Indeed. That is my understanding of it.'

'Reading it now, with the benefit of hindsight, it sounds very much like the kind of note someone might write if they intended to take their own life,' Vita said. 'Do you think she killed herself?'

'I do not,' said the chef. 'She was a religious woman. She would consider that a sin.'

*I*n the parlour a little later, Tante Gabrielle sat with her feet on a low stool listening and taking in the view as Adelina played the piano.

'You think us too light-hearted, Vita,' the larger aunt said, pouring her a cup of tea. 'It would be terribly wrong to play music if it were not for the fact that our darling girl is so much better this morning. She has taken a little breakfast and is sitting up in bed. Of course, she is not fully recovered. That may take a good while yet, she has such a naturally delicate constitution, but her colour is good and she is talking to us. Dr Zecker believes the danger is passed. So we celebrate with a little music.'

Adelina was a good pianist, filling the room with what seemed to be a jolly polka, she was enjoying herself at the keyboard, playing energetically, with playful flourishes of her hands.

'We shall probably be leaving today,' Gabrielle went on. 'Dr Zecker will soon decide whether our dear Lotti is well enough to travel. If she is, we will go to our friends in

London for a few days' convalescence before we travel back to Germany.'

'And has Lotti spoken to ... anyone outside the family?' Vita worded her question tactfully.

Gabrielle shook her head. 'She is with Dr Zecker at the moment. She has seen nobody else. She did not wish it. She is so sensitive, you know.'

Vita did not know what to say to this. 'She has communicated, though? With Alexander?'

'She has been too indisposed to do so.'

'I only mention it because he has been so very anxious about her.'

'Yes. No doubt.' Gabrielle said no more. Adelina completed her jovial polka piece and began to search the piano stool for more music.

Gabrielle leaned in to Vita, profiting from her sister's back being turned. 'Just between us, Vita, I do not think matters are on a good footing between the love birds.'

Vita wanted to ask more, but Adelina had already found another piece of music and was beginning to play again.

'We asked you to join us so that you could tell us about what has been happening. There have been occurrences, goings-on, happenings in the house, yes? We asked Dr Zecker, but he is so discreet. He does not talk about other patients. He only said someone in the household had been taken ill. He did not say who it was. Do you know, Vita?'

Vita gave herself a moment to think by pouring more tea for the aunts, and did the job slowly, carrying a cup to Adelina at the piano and carefully handing one to Gabrielle who fussily stirred three teaspoons of sugar into it for her nerves, as she explained. Whatever the condition of her nerves, she was not to be distracted. 'Well, Vita?'

'It was a member of the staff,' she said, unwillingly.

'A maid? Not the red-haired girl who brings our hot water - I thought she looked peaky, Adelina, I told you so.'

'No, it was the governess.'

'Oh,' Gabriella appeared a little disappointed by this news. 'I think I know the one. I saw her with the little boy. The thin, pale woman who always wears brown.'

Tante Adelina interrupted her playing to pick up her cup and saucer. From the piano she said, 'She did not look healthy, I thought. Is she recovered now?'

Vita hesitated. Both aunts looked at her. At first their look was mildly curious, but the hesitation made both become sharpened and attentive.

'I regret to say that she has died,' Vita finally told them. She did not feel it was right for her to tell them, but on the other hand nobody else seemed to have thought to do so.

The older ladies now looked at one another and spoke in rapid German. 'Was it a contagion? Why have we not been told? Was it the shellfish poisoning? In God's name we must leave this house as rapidly as possible. Did Dr Zecker attend her? If he did he may have brought the contagion with him and spread to it to dear Lotti!'

By now the ladies were beginning to flutter in their anxiety, their voices tremulous and rising in pitch. Vita, in an attempt to quell the upswell of nervous tension, could only spread her hands.

'There is really nothing to fear. I saw Miss Hartley...'

'... You too have been close to her?'

'I accompanied the doctors in their examination. They needed me to translate.'

'How dreadful for you!'

'No, I was perfectly willing.'

'But why? This is not the sort of thing a young lady should be involved with. Think of your own health! Think of your nerves! The strain may damage your health irreparably. I have know such cases ... and that is without even considering the risk of contagion and the dreadful effects of the unhealthy air that may be surrounding you in a sickroom.'

'No, really, I was calm throughout. It was no great strain. Although, of course it was not the easiest task.'

'And what did the poor lady have? What did the doctors say? Not typhus fever - oh do say it was not typhus fever!'

'Please reassure yourselves, it was not a fever that killed Miss Hartley.'

'What then? The oysters! I knew it! They have killed someone. Oh my poor, poor Lotti!'

'Dr Mills had been treating Miss Hartley for general ill health for some time, apparently. She had a condition and it seemed to have taken a sudden turn for the worse, but there was no reason to connect it with the seafood or anything else she had eaten.'

The aunts looked a little calmer.

'I do not trust this Mills, this English doctor. Excuse me, Vita, I am sure there are excellent English doctors, but in the countryside less so. This Mills looks like a farmer. He is rough in his manners and comes and goes in a cart with a plough horse. I have seen him in his muddy boots.'

'He is well known to the family. They have consulted him for many years.' Vita said, surprised to find herself defending Dr Mills.

'Well, I suppose there is nothing better around here.' Gabriella gestured in a sweep wave of her arm across the wide panorama on view from the grand windows.

'I believe it was a self-killing.' Tante Adelina suddenly said. She closed the lid of the piano quietly.

'Why do you say that?' Gabriella asked. Her tea cup rattling in its saucer as she held it in a trembling hand.

'I heard the maids talking,' Adelina told them. 'My English is better than people think. I heard the two girls who came to bring my water and open the curtains chattering. They thought she had killed herself because of a broken heart.'

Gabriella frowned in severe disapproval of this. 'She was far too old for that sort of thing.'

'A woman is not too old for love after she is past the earliest blooming of her youth,' Adelina replied with dignity, replacing the sheet music in the piano stool and bringing her tea over to join them.

Gabriella pursed her lips and shuddered. 'I consider it inappropriate even to discuss such a matter. A governess killing herself for love, indeed! Whoever heard of such a thing in a well-run household. Most unsuitable!'

'Then let us not discuss it further,' Adelina answered.

CHAPTER 34

'Would you say Pemberton was a place of secrets, generally?' Vita asked her aunt.

They were in the small sitting room next to her aunt's bedroom. Louisa had set up her easel by the window and was examining the half completed portrait of Lotti and Alexander.

'Why do you ask that?' Louisa asked. She stepped back and peered at the painting with her head on one side.

'I suppose it's superstitious of me, but it now seems full of undercurrents and hidden things. I heard the housekeeper speaking very harshly to one of the nursery maids this morning. The sound came down the chimney in the Yellow Room. It was as clear as if they had been in the room with me.'

Louisa continued her scrutiny of the painting with a look of displeasure.

'Has Lady Pemberton mentioned a man called Billings?' Vita asked.

'She has. Dickie Pemberton's valet. He is very important to Dickie's health, but rather domineering in the sick room, apparently. Why?'

'I overheard an argument between Billings and Miss

Hartley. He sounded angry. She seemed to owe him money. I saw her collect a bottle from a hidden shelf in the library and he came later for the money she left.'

Louisa's attention turned rapidly to her niece. 'That sounds very strange,' her aunt remarked.

'I think I also saw Miss Hartley once before. In Cambridge. I was in a pharmacy and she came in and tried to bargain with the man behind the counter for more medicine than she could pay for.'

'Miss Hartley? Are you certain?'

'Yes. It took me a while to place her, but now I am certain. I couldn't see what she was buying, but she was truly desperate to have it.'

Her aunt looked at Vita seriously. 'What do you think it might be, this medicine?'

'I imagined some sort of pain relieving mixture. My mother took laudanum for several years, as you know. It was the only medicine that gave her relief.'

'You think Hartley was in pain herself? One can readily become habituated to these medicines. I have known several ladies myself …' She interrupted her thought and began packing her painting and easel away.

'I don't know,' Vita said. 'I may have been the last person to speak to her last night. She told me she had suffered misery and rejection, and in her letter to Monsieur Picard …'

'Which letter?'

'The one I saw her deliver.'

'You know its contents?'

'I met the chef in the garden just now and he showed it to me. It was full of sadness and regret. It was pitiful. When I was with the doctors they agreed that her health had not been good for a long time. Her whole jaw was inflamed on one

132

side and showed infections and possibly abscesses of her teeth.'

Aunt Louisa's hand went unconsciously to her own jaw. 'Oh, the poor woman. Toothache!'

'Of the worst kind,' Vita said, 'and over a long period.'

The very thought of it silenced them both briefly.

'I have only had bad toothache on one occasion,' her aunt said. 'I think it is the worst pain I have ever endured. I would have taken laudanum - or anything else, frankly - to cure it. Luckily, your uncle was on hand and he suggested whisky, which worked very well. But poor Miss Hartley had no kind husband.'

'And laudanum is far cheaper than whisky,' Vita said. 'But she couldn't easily afford it even then. I wonder whether Billings has been profiteering from her urgent need for it? Perhaps he bought it from that dingy chemist and knew he could charge Miss Hartley any price. She has almost no possessions in her room. No jewellery, no little ornaments. I wonder whether she sold them all to buy the medicine.'

'Dear me,' was all Louisa could say, 'What a rat's nest you are conjuring up. Surely this is all rather far-fetched.'

She came over and sat beside her niece. 'We shall need to pass your thoughts on to Felicity. They may help to explain Miss Hartley's death. Felicity is tortured by all that has happened.'

'She was certainly worried about Pemberton and the family's reputation, when she spoke to me,' Vita said.

Her aunt looked over. 'You imply that she was not concerned about Miss Hartley?'

'I'm sorry, Aunt, but she did not express any interest in Miss Hartley at all and even seemed surprised that her children might be affected by their governess's death.'

'Oh come,' Aunt Louisa said, 'that is unkind.'

'What is unkind is to allow a member of the household to be neglected to the point where she endures long periods of poor health with no-one to turn to, in my opinion,' Vita replied.

'Vita! Felicity is one of my oldest friends! You have no right to rush to such a judgement.'

'Perhaps you are right. It is a hasty judgement. My information is incomplete.'

'Vita! That is a ridiculous idea. You have no need of 'information'.'

'Aunt, Miss Hartley has nobody to speak for her. Her death is nothing but an inconvenience to this household. Would you want me to stand by and watch as it is brushed aside?'

'Nobody is trying to brush it aside. Come now. You are tired. You need to rest and take your mind off these difficult events.'

'I heard someone mention an old rhyme about Pemberton,' Vita said.

'The one that begins *Rule at Pemberton*?'

'Yes! You know it?'

'It's very well known. It's just some bit of doggerel carved on a medieval stone they found somewhere.'

'I'm foolish to think about it, I suppose,' Vita said, but it's been playing on my mind. *Rule at Pemberton, rich and well fed; Serve at Pemberton, early dead.* It gives me the creeps.'

'You're tired, I imagine, Dear,' her aunt said, 'it's all been very trying.'

CHAPTER 35

They heard an accented voice outside asking directions of a maid. It was Doctor Zecker. Having knocked and bowed with great formality to both ladies, he addressed Vita.

'I should like to discuss this morning's observations. Could you bring your notes to the library? If you would permit this, of course, Frau Brocklehurst.'

'My niece is not to be overstrained by her translating duties, Doctor Zecker. She is very young. She has already been exposed to too many distressing details.'

Dr Zecker bowed humbly in consent, which Aunt Louisa, who was ready to go to battle, found rather disarming.

'Your niece's note-taking was exemplary,' he said. 'I hoped only for the briefest discussion.'

'Very well. But Vita is not to be overburdened. And I think it would be more suitable for your conversation to take place in my presence.'

'Of course,' the doctor said.

'My notes are in my room, but I need a few minutes to finish copying them,' Vita told him.

'Then I have time to call in on Fraulein Von Diepentahl, who was feeling stronger when last I saw her. I shall return in thirty minutes.'

Smiling and bowing, Dr Zecker backed out of the room.

'What an odd little person he is,' Louisa remarked. 'I never feel comfortable with men whose age is mysterious. Do you? He could be twenty-five or forty.'

Vita followed Dr Zecker out of the room and was surprised to find him waiting on the landing outside.

'Why did you catch my eye, when Dr Mills asked me to hand over my notes earlier?' she asked as he fell into step beside her.

Dr Zecker smiled, but did not answer. 'Tell me first about your interest in science, Miss Carew.'

Vita was irritated by this obvious diversion. 'I simply find scientific subjects of interest. My father is a naturalist. I enjoy observing his methods.'

'But you have not studied formally?'

'No. I had a governess, she was Swiss, which is how I learnt German and French. She left after Mama became unwell. After that my education came to an end.'

'Did you regret this?'

'I was greatly occupied with nursing my mother. And after Mama died, I helped my father with his parish work. There was always a lot to be done.'

'Please accept my sincere condolences on the loss of your mother, Miss Carew. But your brother continued his studies?'

'Yes, with some success. He won a scholarship to Trinity College.'

'Surely you are tempted to study yourself?'

'I try to read my brother's textbooks, but I find them very difficult to understand. I lack a fundamental grounding in the science subjects. I cannot understand even basic principles.'

They passed the suit of armour. Partly as a way of changing the subject, Vita stood to attention and saluted. Zecker watched, raised an eyebrow, but then joined her salute.

'In Germany,' he said, as they set off again, 'women can graduate exactly as men. We had two women students among us when I studied Medicine.'

'Two? Really?'

'Indeed yes. In my country women can qualify as medical doctors, just as men do.'

'That is not possible here.'

Zecker shrugged. 'We are more advanced in Germany, I think,' he said, with a small smile. 'But, to the business in hand: I should like a chance to read the notes before they are handed to Dr Mills.'

'You fear my errors?'

'Not in the least. I wish to add a few of my own observations, that is all. Doctor Mills may not agree with my thoughts, but I should like them recorded. Ah, here we have the staircase I must follow to my patient. We will meet again shortly, yes?'

The German doctor peeled off and galloped down the stairs at a surprising speed.

CHAPTER 36

*A*pproaching the Yellow Bedroom, Vita heard voices. The door was ajar. Putting her ear to the opening she could hear enough to identify Billings and Mrs Parks. Papers rustled. They were looking at her notes and speaking in urgent undertones.

'What's it say about where they found her?' Billings asked.

'She was on the floor, it says. Near the door.'

'You said you put her in bed.'

'I did. I thought she was just drunk at first.'

'Did she smell of the drink?'

'I tried to see if she was drawing breath, but I couldn't tell. Not for sure. Then I thought, Oh Lord in Heaven, she's dead. I couldn't think straight. I just put her in bed, so I could think about what to do.'

'All you cared about was keeping it quiet. You didn't want to disturb the beautiful music or the engagement or the posh dinner. You didn't care if she was dead or alive.' Billings said this with a sneer.

'I thought the woman was dead, Billings! There was no

harm in leaving her a bit longer. Why ruin everything we've spent months preparing?'

'Only she wasn't dead, was she, Mrs Parks?'

'Yes she was!'

'How'd she move then? You saying she got up out of bed *after* she was dead?'

A brief silence fell. When she spoke again there was a new, fearful tone to the housekeeper's voice.

'Will they get the police? What am I going to do? Dear God, Billings, they'll hang me.'

'No they won't. You didn't kill her. You just...'

'I left her to die. I thought she was dead already. But she wasn't. I left that poor woman to die. God help me. I never meant to.'

'You just keep steady. I'll make sure you're kept out of this,' Billings said. 'But you've got to read the next part of it. Does it say anything in there about bottles?'

'Bottles?'

'Medicine bottles?'

'No, it says she was on the floor, she had bad teeth, the room was almost empty, she was dead. That's all. Some words are foreign. It must be German.'

'German?'

'The girl - the one who wrote this, she's written some of the words in German.'

'What's she done that for? Hiding things?'

'You'll have to ask her that.'

'Is there nothing in there about medicine? Or blue bottles?'

'No. What blue bottles?'

'I done her a favour a few times. I give her some of his Lordship's medicine.'

'What? Why did you do that?'

'She suffered with her teeth. It was bad.'

'You were making money out of her!'

'Not much, just a small amount for my trouble. I only give her one bottle at a time - it's dangerous. It says poison on the label.'

'How do you know what it says? We all know you can't read well.'

'I'm not stupid. It has a skull and crossbones on it. That's poison. I give her one bottle at a time. Thirty drops in milk, that's the right amount. She has to give it back before I give her another. I made sure she didn't take too much. Like I do with his Lordship.'

'Thirty drops? That would depend on the strength of it. If you can't read, you wouldn't know the right dose, would you?'

'He always gives me the same. I know the man at the pharmacy. What do you know about laudanum anyway?'

'I've worked in big houses for thirty years. You think I've never seen opium before? I reckon it might be your doing. You told her to take too much of it. That would kill her. Anyway, you don't need to worry about the bottle because I took it away. There was one on her night stand and I put it in my pocket.'

'Where is it now then?'

'I put it in the bottle room in the cellar.'

Vita was trying to make sense of what she was hearing when an urgent call rang out along the hallway and the running footsteps of a housemaid were heard on the stairs. She was taking the fastest route up the stairs in the blocked-off end of the corridor.

'Mr Billings! His Lordship is ringing for you.'

Billings and Mrs Parks were out of the Yellow Bedroom in seconds. Billings hurried towards the maid. The housekeeper hurried in the other direction and disappeared down the stairs. Neither saw Vita who had slipped into the shadows further up the landing.

In the Yellow Room Vita found her notes on the table. They were disordered, but complete.

CHAPTER 37

'*I* observed that the deceased had about her lips a very slight powdery deposit, suggesting that she had taken a medicine or drunk something which was a powder suspension.' Dr Zecker paced the room as he dictated. He paused to allow Vita to translate his words and write them.

'The patient was extremely underweight. This combination of observations lead me to wonder whether she was not taking regular doses of a sedative medicine. Perhaps one intended to cure toothache, as she also showed clear signs, in the swelling of her jaw, of a dental infection.'

'Do I speak too fast, Miss Carew?'

'No, I am keeping up,' said Vita, writing.

'In addition to this, I was concerned that there appeared to have been an effort to clear Miss Hartley's room of possessions. It was conspicuously empty of the usual mementoes and personal belongings a woman of her age might have been expected to accumulate. There was scarcely a photograph, a painting or even a postcard to be seen. Even in a woman of severe tastes, this seems unusual. It suggests that someone cleared her room before we were called to attend her.'

'Why should someone clear her room?' asked Aunt Louisa from behind her easel. She was working on the portrait again.

'To conceal things, or possibly to steal them, I imagine,' the doctor told her.

'But what needed to be hidden? What motive could they have for hiding things? It was the housekeeper who found her. You are suggesting that the housekeeper took things from her room? Why should she do this?' Louisa's tone was irritated.

Dr Zecker shrugged. 'I cannot say. It is difficult to find an explanation.'

At this moment Swain opened the library door and showed Dr Mills in. Without acknowledging the ladies, the English doctor said, 'You are discussing the case?'

'I was just saying to Miss Carew that I believed the governess's room must have been cleared of personal possessions before we arrived.'

Vita translated.

'Why do you say so?' Mills demanded.

'It was so bare. Nobody has so few personal possessions.'

'The staff believe she sold them,' Mills said. He was slightly flushed and now produced a large handkerchief and wiped his face. 'Below stairs they believe she had debts and was pawning or selling her valuables. Either that or she was attempting to accumulate a fund for another purpose. Perhaps she had it in mind to travel somewhere.'

The thought of the governess, as she had last seen her, doing something as cheerful as planning a journey struck Vita as extremely unlikely, but she translated Mills's words.

'I am concerned, also, with the advanced state of the rigor

that we observed,' Zecker continued. 'When the police attend, I shall ...'

'...Why should the police attend?' Mills interrupted. 'There is no need to bother them. I am her doctor and I shall certify her death.'

Vita and the German doctor looked in amazement at Mills, who was settling himself on one of the low sofas. The aunts were correct about his boots being muddy, Vita noticed.

'Now listen here. I have attended Miss Hartley for a number of years. She has not been in good health since last winter. I treated her then and have seen her several times since. She has been suffering from poor health in general, with lack of appetite and difficulty in sleeping. Her spirits have been low as a result. There was a general deterioration over several months. I expect to record congestive pulmonary weakness as the cause of death.'

'But you will ask for a post-mortem examination of a more extensive and detailed kind, yes? In order that you can be certain?' Zecker said.

'Not at all. As I said, I have seen this patient regularly and I have no reason to suspect anything other than natural causes for her death.'

'I find this most irregular.'

'Perhaps you do things differently in Germany, but here in England a medical man's opinion is respected when one of his patients dies. There is no need whatever to go to the officious lengths of a police surgeon's post mortem examination.'

Vita's translation skills were being strained to the utmost by this conversation.

'And what do you make of the evident signs of her having taken some medicine or draught of some kind? There were no bottles or glasses to be seen. They had been removed. Somebody, I believe, had cleared her room of these things after her death.'

'I am familiar with this household, Dr Zecker. Nobody would do such a thing. Nor would anyone lie about what happened.'

'She had been dead longer than a few hours, though. You must agree. So advanced a state of rigor would not have been possible if she had only died in the small hours of the night before.'

'It was a cold room. We both noted that. You must be well aware that the state of rigor is highly unpredictable. Different medical conditions affect it. The temperature affects it, and so on. I have no such reservations.'

'And what of the swelling on her jaw? Will you do no more to investigate that?'

'What is the point of establishing whether a dead woman had toothache?' Mills said. 'Ada Hartley was in poor health and now she has died. It is a pity, but I see no advantage in pursuing the details of the matter any further. I shall sign the death certificate and the funeral arrangements will be set in train immediately.'

'And you have no concern that in not investigating whether she was suffering from poisoning you may be missing some vital information that will help in the recovery of the other patients?'

'The other patients? There is in fact only one now, Miss ... the German singer ... her name escapes me for a moment - is making a good recovery. There is no reason to imagine a connection between the governess and the unfortunate events at the dinner. I can see no advantage in carrying out unnecessary investigations on the unfortunate Miss Hartley.'

Zecker bristled, but only said, 'This is not how such matters are dealt with in Germany.'

'Perhaps so, but we are not in Germany now,' said Mills.

To Vita he then said, 'I will not be discussing this matter any further with Dr Zecker. Tell him that. As far as I am concerned his involvement in this matter is now superfluous. I would recommend that he limit himself to the care of Miss ... of his own patient. Make sure he understands that.'

Vita translated and observed the effect of this statement on Zecker. The insult had clearly hit home.

'But what of the cause of the food poisoning? Will you do nothing to investigate this?' the German asked.

'Investigate? What is there to investigate? It was a bad lot of French oysters,' Mills said. 'It's hardly even unusual.'

'How do you know this? How does he know this? He has not taken any samples or carried out any tests!' Zecker, fizzing with irritation, seemed now to be speaking to Vita. She wasn't sure whether to translate, but need not have worried as Mills was no longer listening. He had walked to the door. There he looked over his shoulder and addressed his last remark to Vita.

'I should avoid the man from now on, if I were you. He is misguided in his ideas and seems to want to disrupt our whole way of doing things here. Take my advice: shake him off as soon as you can. There must be more entertaining occupations than acting as translator for aristocratic Germans and their ridiculous tame doctors.' He stomped to the door and threw it open. 'I'll bid you good day. I have patients waiting in town. I consider this matter at an end.'

Zecker drew himself up and marched out of the room pausing only to bow to Aunt Louisa and Vita as he passed.

'Well! That was quite an encounter,' Aunt Louisa remarked, rinsing her paintbrush and drying it on her apron. I think I shall ring for a little sherry, I need something to restore my nerves.' She pulled the embroidered cord by the fireplace. 'From what I understood the doctors are in dispute over the cause of the unfortunate Miss Hartley's death?'

'Yes. As you heard, Dr Mills sees no reason for the police to be involved. She died of natural causes, as he sees it.'

'Clearly Dr Zecker disagrees.'

'He believes she was taking opium medicine and possibly that is what caused her death. I have just overheard something that might confirm his ideas.'

'And the police? I heard Mills saying they weren't needed. Felicity would certainly rather keep the police out of the matter.'

Louisa stood and looked out of window. Below, Dr Mills in a raincoat with caped shoulders billowing, climbed into his rough little carriage, flicked the reins and drove away, the wheels spraying rain. Even the horse looked angry.

'And Vita, what is your view of all this?'

At her aunt's side Vita could only shake her head.

'There are some details about Miss Hartley's death that are hard to explain. Dr Zecker is right about that.'

'Which details?'

'The signs suggested she had died a long time before.'

'But surely that is just because nobody found her.'

'Her room was so cold and empty,' Vita said.

'The fire had gone out. But I agree it is odd that she had so few belongings. Felicity told me in confidence that Miss Hartley was suspected by the staff of stealing. Small items went missing and were occasionally found in her room.'

'There was nothing there this morning. It truly was bare.'

Both women continued to look out at the rain gusting across the formal gardens and deer park beyond. 'There was something pitiful about Hartley, wasn't there?' Aunt Louisa said.

'Yes, there was. She advised me never to become a governess.'

'Did she say why not?'

'I would end up unwanted and despised.'

'Dear me. Just as well you have no such plans then Vita, my dear. Now where is that sherry?'

Vita pulled off her glasses and polished the lenses on a fold of her skirt. 'I have no particular talents and very few funds,' she said, 'becoming a governess is not out of the question. It may be my only choice.'

'Oh come now,' said her aunt. 'That is a very old-fashioned view, Vita. You are an intelligent young woman. Earning an independent living is not impossible these days. At something other than being a governess, I mean.'

'Not without some sort of training or aptitude.'

'You have plenty of aptitude, Vita. Look at how useful the doctors find you. They have nothing but praise. The German aunts too, are delighted by your attentiveness to them.'

'Yes. I am generally helpful - this does not qualify me to make a living.'

'You take an interested in science,' said her aunt.

'A vague general interest in something does not qualify me to make a living either, though.'

'Oh dear, you have taken poor Miss Hartley's words to heart, haven't you? I shall have to ring again for that sherry.'

BUT THE NEXT knock on the door brought an urgent summons, not the hoped-for sherry.

'The master is took ill, Miss. Lady Felicity asks you to come and speak for the German doctor.'

Vita followed the maid down to the basement, along the servants' passage and up a steep flight of stairs she had not noticed before. It took them to a dim landing where the maid knocked on a wooden panel which was swiftly opened from the inside by a footman. They were in Lord Pemberton's dressing room.

CHAPTER 39

As Vita stepped inside, Dr Zecker, helped by a footman, was lifting the master's unconscious body with some difficulty from the floor onto the narrow bed at the centre of the room. Vita was struck by the lack of decoration in this room. It seemed to have been partitioned from one much larger. The grand height of its ceiling was out of proportion with its meagre floor space and single narrow window. Intricate plaster mouldings, once gold leafed but now faded and peeling, were interrupted by new walls. The furniture was plain and even the bed was narrow. It looked more like a servant's attic room than a master's private chamber.

'Ah, Miss Carew,' Zecker said, 'I would like you to ask this man, I forget his name, this one who attends the gentleman ...'

'You mean Billings?'

'Yes, he. Please ask him when he found his master and what medicines Lord Pemberton has taken.'

Billings, pale and looking fixedly at the bed, was holding

the back of a chair as if he would fall without it. She relayed this question.

He seemed to take a moment to tear his attention from the prone figure of his master, then answered, 'I found him on the floor. I thought he had just fallen from the bed, but I could not rouse him. I thought he was…'

'What medicine has he taken?' Zecker repeated. Vita translated.

'Only his usual sleeping medicine,' Billings replied.

'In heaven's name what drug is in this medicine?'

Vita translated this question, but Billings only shrugged. 'Laudanum. I give him thirty drops in milk.'

'Where is the bottle?'

'I've thrown it away,' Billings said. 'It was empty, so I took it downstairs.'

'Tell him it is important that I have this bottle so that I can try to confirm the constituents of any remains in it.'

'I have another bottle,' Billings said. He opened a cupboard and produced a blue bottle. Its cork was sealed with wax.

'Does it not have a label?'

'I took it off. It is the same one I always use.'

'But the label tells the dosage.'

'I've seen them enough times. I just take the labels off.'

Zecker turned back to the patient, whose pulse he had been taking during this exchange. He lifted the sleeping man's eyelids and put his ear down to listen to his chest.

'You stay, if you please, Miss Carew. Everyone else should leave.'

Vita conveyed this instruction to the room and the footman left immediately. Billings did not move.

'Tell the man Billings to go to the bottle store and search

for the empty bottle. It is vitally important that it should be found.'

Billings protested at this. 'It is in a large box of bottles. I just tossed it in. I won't be able to find it.'

'He can find it if he tries. He can ask the other footmen to help him, but he must find it immediately,' Zecker said.

Billings, even after this was translated, seemed unwilling to move.

'Billings. Do as you are told,' Lady Felicity spoke for the first time. She had slipped into the room and was standing by the door.

Billings hesitated another moment, then hurried away.

'I shall make sure he is thorough and given help. Vita, you stay with the doctor.'

Lady Pemberton followed Billings, taking the back stairs.

'I am glad she has gone for a few moments. Here, Vita, help me to raise his head. I want to use some harder methods to try to restore his consciousness.'

Zecker then slapped the cheek of the sleeping man, whose head rolled to one side under the blow. There was no other response. Zecker changed sides and slapped the patient again, harder this time. 'Lord Pemberton! Come back! Wake up now!' he shouted into his patient's lolling ear.

'It looks unreasonably violent,' he told Vita, 'but I can assure you it is the recognised way. He is not completely unconscious. There are reflexes. I want to keep him as wakeful as I can. We do not know what he has taken, though I imagine it is a sleeping draught of the usual concoction with opium and so on. If he has taken too much, he is in danger of falling asleep and not re-awakening. We will do our best to rouse him. Vita, pinch his toe, please. Yes, pinch it hard, the big toe. Try the other one. We must try to keep him awake.'

With the gentlest knock, Swain appeared at the door. He

took in what was happening to his master with the slightest flicker of alarm, but remained composed.

'Ask him for a bucket of cold water and some ice, if it can be found,' Zecker said and once this was translated, Swain immediately disappeared again.

The German doctor continued to shout and slap the patient. 'If we can rouse him, we stand a chance of getting him to drink something to dilute what he has taken.'

Vita hated to see the rough treatment being delivered to the helpless sleeping man. Lord Pemberton's face was a nasty grey and his neck completely lacked the strength to hold his head, which rolled and flopped with every blow. His breathing was ragged and unsteady.

'Pinch his cheek, Miss Carew. Call to him. He must not slip away.'

Swain returned with a bucket of cold water. They soaked towels in it and placed them on the patient's chest and forehead. Zecker, with Swain's help, attempted to get him to swallow a little water, but he was too unresponsive to do so, falling limp as a rag doll back onto the pillow each time.

Lady Pemberton returned to the room. 'The men are all searching for the bottle. They should find it soon.' If she was alarmed by what she saw, she did not show it.

'Tell her ladyship that her voice may help to rouse him. She should call to him and order him to wake up,' Zecker instructed.

'Dickie, my darling. I want you to wake up now,' Felicity told him. 'Wake up and look at us, Dickie. Wake up. We need you with us now.'

Still the head lolled on the pillow. The cheeks now reddened by the slapping they had received, but other wise the face still a corpse-like waxy grey.

Felicity seemed at a loss for a brief moment. She sat back

in a chair and looked miserably around at the butler, the doctor and Vita, but then stood up with new determination and walked to the sick man's bedside.

CHAPTER 40

'*Y*ou shall not leave us, Dickie. I forbid it. You have a wife and children who need you. You shall not desert us. I will not permit you to slip away. I will not allow it! We want you here. You have removed yourself from us for quite long enough over the years. You shall not neglect your duties now. You must wake up and speak to us and return to your family. You are needed, Dickie! Wake up!'

To the astonishment of all, she then picked up the bucket and dashed the rest of the contents over her husband's unconscious form. Whether it was his wife's tone of voice, the shock of the very cold water, or the loud crash of the empty bucket hitting the floor, there was a distinct, if muted response from the patient. He coughed twice and his hands flexed.

'Quickly. We must continue to stimulate him,' Zecker told Vita. 'Pump his arms.' They raised and lowered the man's arms rapidly, as if he were swimming a backstroke. Vita imagined that there was a marginally different muscle tone now, but she could not be certain.

155

'It was the noise that woke him, wasn't it?' Lady Felicity said, and jumping to her feet again she picked up the bucket and threw it with all her strength against the brass rail at the foot of the bed, making an earsplitting noise. In the echoing silence that followed the patient's breathing changed its rhythm. 'You see? He heard that! Perhaps it was the cold water. Swain, please bring some more.' Frantic, she picked the empty bucket up and held it out to the butler, who glanced for confirmation at Dr Zecker.

'I shall need Swain to help lift him to his feet,' Zecker said. With the help of the women, they hauled the still unconscious man to the edge of the bed, then Swain on one side and Zecker on the other took an arm over their shoulder and lifted him upright. Slowly they began dragging him, feet trailing behind, across the room. He seemed almost as lost to them as before, but something indefinable had changed. Felicity walked ahead and when they paused she spoke fiercely to him as before. He must not sleep. He must not abandon his family. His children needed him. She needed him. The house could not run without him. He must wake up!

By the time the slow circuit of the room was completed, the patient seemed to attempt to lift his head. They heard him mutter something and cough. His bare beet struggled to co-operate in the forced walking. He was beginning to regain consciousness.

Within an hour he had taken a little water and could answer a simple question, but keeping him awake was still difficult and Zecker did not want to risk him drifting off again, so they took it in turns to dip cloths in cold water, pinch his toes, slap his cheeks or make noises loud enough to prevent it.

~

Tom and Daniel, both called away from other work, were searching the cellar bottle store with Billings.

'You sure you put it in this one?' Tom said, looking at the mounded contents of one of the large crates of discarded bottles they had emptied onto the flagstoned floor.

'I just threw it,' Billings told them. 'How should I know which one it went in?'

'Why does that German doctor want it, anyhow?' Daniel asked.

'Don't ask me,' Billings said with a shrug.

'He thinks you give the master something bad, I reckon.'

Tom said this straightening up and looking Billings in the eye.

'Don't be daft,' Billings said.

'Did you?'

'Did I what?'

'Give his lordship something that made him take sick like that?'

'Course I bloody didn't.'

'Why'd you hide the bottle, then?'

'I chucked it away. I never hid it. It was just the same medicine he always takes.'

The two young footmen looked severely at Billings.

'He's lying,' Daniel said. 'He's a liar and I reckon he does a bit of thieving too. He creeps around the maids. Now he's gone and poisoned the master.'

He moved behind Billings and closed the wooden door of the glass store. The click of its metal latch made the valet look round.

'Here, what are you ..?'

Without answering, Daniel punched Billings in the face. The valet fell to his knees among the broken glass on the floor, then struggled to stand, but lost his footing and sprawled full length.

Tom had not moved. He stood over Billings and said, 'It'll be a lot worse than that if you don't find that bottle, won't it Daniel?'

'It will. And I'll enjoy doing it, too. You're a nasty piece of work, Billings.'

Billings struggled to sit. He held up a hand, bleeding from several cuts. 'You can't do this. The master'll have you for this,' he said, but his voice, high pitched and fearful, only made them smile.

'We'll finish the job if you don't find that bloody bottle.'

'It's in the corner over there,' Billings muttered. He pointed to a corner away from the crates they had been emptying. A pile of sacking was folded there. 'It's under that lot.'

Daniel went over and pulled the sacks aside. He pulled several small bottles out and held them up.

'Why go to the trouble of hiding them then, Billings?' he said, sniffing the empty bottles and examining them. 'What have you been up to?'

'Nothing. They are just the master's usual sleeping medicine.'

Daniel put several blue bottles in to his pockets.

'Much as I'd enjoy giving him a beating, we should get those bottles to the German doctor pretty quick,' Tom said.

'What shall we do with Billings here?' Daniel asked, poking Billings in the back.

'We could lock him in.'

'The lock's better on the swill room,' said Daniel, sounding suddenly cheerful.

'So it is. This way then, Mr Valet, you can have a nice little rest with the swill buckets.'

They grabbed Billings on each side and dragged him across the stone passage to the room full of stinking bins of pig food.

CHAPTER 41

*V*ita looked from the Yellow Bedroom window along the avenue of trees that stretched into the distance. The children were moving about upstairs. She could hear them in the nursery playroom. Would they know more about Miss Hartley? Did anyone? The governess was little more than an inconvenience in her ill health and in her death. Something to be tidied away. After years of service it was as easy to dispose of her as to throw away a chipped glass or cracked dish.

She had returned to the Yellow Room to fetch a jacket – Pemberton was living up to its reputation for cold, but as she entered the saw a note had been pushed beneath her door. She opened it and saw that it had come from Monsieur Picard.

Dear Miss Carew,

I would be most obliged if you would meet me in the Chef's pantry as soon as possible.

Emile Picard.

She heard footsteps approaching. One of the maids opened the door.

'The German ladies are looking for you, Miss. They are in the parlour.'

Monsieur Picard would have to wait a little longer.

'We are leaving, Vita. But we could not depart without saying goodbye to our little translator, could we, Adelina?'

'Of course not! You have been such a comfort to us in this terrible time, Vita. We are so grateful.'

'Miss Von Diepentahl is well enough to travel now, I take it,' Vita said.

'She is! Of course she must lie down in the carriage, which means Dr Zecker must travel separately, but he assures us she is strong enough for the journey.'

'Please feel free to write to us, Vita,' Tante Gabrielle said.' And if you should ever visit Germany, you must be our guest.' Both the ladies nodded and smiled so enthusiastically that Vita could only agree.

'And we have a little thank you gift!' Adelina added, handing her a package.

It contained a signed handbill for one of Karlotta's concerts which showed a charming drawing of the singer performing before a cheering crowd.

'And take a little advice from a lady who has seen something of the world, Vita,' Gabrielle continued, 'make a little more of your appearance. Something could be done with the hair. And the eyeglasses, well, we have already discussed the eyeglasses.'

Vita smiled on.

So the hair is found wanting too? she thought, after they had finally departed.

～

WILLIAM WAS LEANING on the back of a sofa looking out of the window in the long hall when Vita passed on her way to the chef's basement room.

'Miss Hartley has died now,' he told her, as she approached. 'She was teaching me the piano yesterday, but now she has died.'

'I'm sorry to hear that, William,' Vita said. She took pity on the small, solitary boy, and paused to sit beside him.

He rested his chin on his hands.

'I think she died of happiness.' The boy said suddenly. He still did not look at her, but directed his remarks towards the window. 'Miss Hartley told me she would die of happiness if she heard the singing. I heard her in her room last night. I think she was dancing. You could hear the music a little bit, even in my room. It was nice music. Can someone die of happiness?'

Vita looked at the boy, for a few moments, unable to formulate an answer. *If that is what dying of happiness looks like,* she thought, *I hope I never see the body of someone who has died of misery and distress.*

'They're going to send Netty away too,' William continued, 'I like her, but she keeps crying and crying. Mama says Mrs Parks will have to send her away. Someone else will make tea for Mary-Ann and me now. And give us our medicine at bedtime. But a good thing is that I am to go to school and Mary-Ann too. We are glad about that. We will have lots of friends at school. My cousin is there. He says it's ripping good fun. I can take Blackstock, that's my pony.'

As the boy spoke, Vita saw the figure of Billings come up the stairs further along. Even from a distance she could tell he was in a rage. His clothes were untidy and his movements clumsy. He saw her talking to William and turned in their direction.

'William, I want you to go and find Swain, please. Go now, and ask him to come here as quickly as you can. Take the other staircase. Hurry William.'

The boy looked confused for a moment, then hurried off.

CHAPTER 42

*V*ita considered escaping herself, but Billings was already hailing her.

'It's you that got this started,' he called. 'What's it to you anyway? You never even knew the governess! What's any of it got to do with you?'

'I don't know what you mean,' Vita told him, trying to keep her voice calm. He was a large man, red-faced in fury and ready to fight. As he approached the rank smell of pigswill followed. His jacket was ripped at the shoulder and dried blood crusted at the corner of his mouth.

'Your German lies. That's what did it.'

'German lies? What do you mean?'

'Why'd you write secrets in German then? To hide things? Come with me,' he said. He lunged, took her arm in a painful grip and began to drag her to the main staircase.

'Let me go,' Vita said, trying to free her arm, but he was far stronger, hauling her up two flights and across a landing to a smaller stone stair beyond. Up these steps they continued, Vita's feet tripping and stumbling as they narrowed and twisted upward. An arched wooden door gave onto a stone turret room. Billings dragged Vita in, closed the door behind them and leaned against it panting.

'Tell me what you wrote in those notes you made about the body. What did the doctors say and why was it in German? What did they say killed her? She never did it, Mrs Parks. She just found her and moved her. She never gave her medicine. I gave her medicine, but only the normal bottle she always had. It wouldn't kill her. That wasn't it.'

He was making no sense to Vita. She heard only an outpouring of incoherent words. 'Why have you brought me here?' she asked, trying, once again to speak quietly and sound as calm as she could.

Billings turned and reached into a corner where a small wooden cupboard was fixed to the curving stone wall. He opened it with a key and showed her the contents - several rows of small blue bottles. 'I keep them here. I wanted you to see them. They are not harmful. They are all the same. The chemist makes them for his Lordship. I keep them here under lock and key. Safe. I count the drops out. Same every night. It wasn't me that made his Lordship ill. It wasn't me that killed Hartley. They both took this medicine. They liked it and it did both of them good.'

'I know about Laudanum, Billings, my mother took it. I gave it to her.'

'Then you know how sick people need it. It's a blessing to them. I've done nothing wrong. Whatever you wrote in your German, I've done nothing wrong, see?'

He was angry again.

'May I look at the bottles?' Vita asked.

'They're all the same,' he said.

'Why did you remove their labels?'

'I didn't need to see them. It's always the same. Generally I just take them off and put them in the fire.'

165

Vita stood up slowly. 'Can I look?' she asked.

'I want you to. That's why I brought you up here. You'll see I haven't done anything wrong. Look at them.'

The smell of him in the small circular room was almost overpowering. His clothes stank of old meat and rotting vegetables and the sweat that was beading his face.

Vita peered into the dark cupboard. At the very back some bottles did still have brown labels tied to their necks. She reached in and pulled two of them out.

'On that side, they're the new ones. I got them Friday,' Billings told her. 'That other one is older. I keep them in order. I take care. You can give it to babies. The chemist told me people give it to babies to help them sleep. It's well-made, carefully mixed. I wouldn't give it to them otherwise. I'm helping them.'

'How much does Lord Pemberton take?'

'Thirty or forty drops. Sometimes a bit more. He asks for more.'

'Billings, that is a great deal of this medicine. It says 'poisonous in excess'.'

'I know that,' Billings said, annoyed. 'He needs that much to take his pain off.'

'These new bottles are a stronger mix than usual,' Vita said. 'It says it on the label here. They are twice as strong. If someone takes their normal dose, they are really taking twice as much as before.'

'No. It's the same.'

'It isn't the same, Billings.'

'You're wrong. You're making it up. You and your German secrets. Your lies. You'll lose me my job.'

A thought suddenly occurred to Vita. 'Did you give any of this new batch to anyone else?'

'Only Netty,' he said.

'Netty? The nursery maid? Why?'

'For the boy. He doesn't sleep well. He gets it at bedtime to send him off.'

Vita felt her knees weaken beneath her at the thought of little William being dosed with these wretched medicine. Billings was quieter now. He was struggling to take in the implications of the label on the small bottle in Vita's hand.

'Billings. It's very important that nobody gives this to William. Do you understand?'

'It won't harm him. You can give it to babies.'

'Not this kind. It's not mixed correctly. This is dangerous. Please let me go and...'

'It's not dangerous! I told you it's not dangerous!' Roused to sudden fury he lunged toward Vita, grabbing at her collar, causing her glasses to fly from her face and fall to the stone floor. He pulled her towards him and hissed in her face, 'I've done nothing wrong. You'll tell them and get me in trouble. I'll stop you. You're just a busybody. Nobody thinks you're clever, you and your German...'

He was jerking her from side to side, his hot, rank breath on her face. He stamped a foot and Vita distinctly heard the splinter of trampled spectacles.

'Billings, please! The boy doesn't deserve to die.'

He was holding her at the throat, her blouse twisted too tightly. She was beginning to feel the pressure of blood in her neck and face. She lost her footing and the pressure grew even stronger as he put his hands around her neck and, twisting his face with the effort, began to squeeze.

As she fell, Vita felt the valet pulled off balance. His grip was still tight and the pulse loud in her ears, but she summoned a surge of powerful determination at the thought of the children. She must protect the children from this medicine. She had to get to them. Scrabbling furiously, she kicked with all her strength, aiming for Billings' soft middle parts, repeatedly pounding her boot heels as viciously as she could. He roared. His grasp on her neck shifted. She was able to catch a breath, but he was still by far the stronger.

The children. I must get to the children. Again the thought pushed fear aside and brought Vita a new burst of strength. She reached toward the blur that was probably Billings' head and grabbed for hair and ears. He shouted in pain again. There were other sounds too. Her own howls – of effort and rage more than fear – echoed around the circular stone room.

It was exhausting work, this fighting, a distant part of her brain recorded.

The children. Miss Hartley's thin dead corpse with its vacant death grin came to her again. William and Mary-Ann must not take the drug – the one that must have killed their governess.

Something was in her hand. A bottle. She grasped it and swung her fist as hard as she could towards her attacker's face. She felt the glass thud into his jaw.

CHAPTER 43

*A*s she hit the cold stone floor, Vita heard the crash of the door thrown back and the shouts of several men. At first they seemed distant, as though her ears were full of water. She could see black shapes flailing and hear Billings bellow with rage. She was jerked to her feet, his arm now around her neck from behind. His voice close to her ear he shouted, 'I'll kill her, I swear I'll kill her if you come any closer.'

Vita's struggle to breathe took all her energy. Her feet were barely on the ground, her neck was pulled back. She could smell the stink of rotten cabbage on the arm of Billings's jacket. Her mind swirled with the angry thought that there must – *there must* – be something she could do to defend herself, if only she could *think*.

Billings, holding her like a shield between himself and the men, barged past them and dragged Vita behind him up the last flight of stairs to the top of the turret. It was twisting and narrow, too narrow for anyone to do more than follow. The small door at the top, which he barged with his shoulder, opened to an icy blast of air. They were at roof height, ahead only a narrow walkway between the steep slope of the Hall's roof and the crumbling stonework of ancient battlements. Vita, resisting but breathless and losing the focus of her thoughts, glimpsed the sheer drop of fifty feet to the wet gravel of the carriage drive below.

'Why are we here?' she shouted, but her voice was muffled in the freezing air. 'What do you want?'

'To keep you quiet, you and your lies,' Billings growled. 'To shut you up for good and all.'

There were shouts from the men giving chase.

'Billings, let her go! Down! Get down, Miss!'

The men had reached the turret door. One was crawling onto the walkway. He had a stick. At first their words were lost, but Billings, shocked himself by the cold and the terrifying height, loosened his grip on Vita's neck for a fraction of second. She gulped icy air. Out across the rooftop she glimpsed a wide view: rolling cloud and steely sleet-blown sky.

The cold air cleared her mind. She fell to her knees, slipping through Billings' grip, and threw herself down along the walkway. It felt better to be lower than the parapet. In fury Billings lunged forward, grabbing for her. The faces of the chasing footmen were pale behind him in the dark doorway. They shouted helpless warnings, but it was too late. Billings' feet scrabbled in the grit of broken stonework and he lost his balance, flailing his arms and falling heavily across the low peaked block of a castellation. For a fateful moment he clung to it, his head and shoulders jutting over the drop. Then, with Vita and the men watching helplessly, the brickwork cracked along the base, tipped, shifted, then fell away. With a short grunt of shock and fear Billings rolled over with it and plunged out of sight.

For the space of a breath the footmen and Vita were frozen, then all heard the sickening impact below.

Tom, on hands and knees, reached and helped Vita crawl back to the safety of the turret. Swain took her arm. The younger men ran down to raise the alarm.

'Are you hurt, Miss?'

'I don't think so. I only need to get my breath. Did he fall? Is he dead? He'll be dead, won't he?'

The shock was making Vita feel sick. Her hands were trembling. The sound they had both heard, of Billings' body meeting the ground, was still echoing in her memory. She tossed her head, as if to shake it from her ears.

'The men will fetch help, Miss, Dr Mills has been called for already,' Swain told her, guiding her round the twisting stone stairs.

Vita could only manage small thoughts. 'Oh, Swain,' she said, 'my glasses. I think he destroyed them.'

Swain led her down to the room below and retrieved the misshapen frame of a small pair of glasses from the floor. Neither eyepiece had a lens.

'I'm afraid you are correct there, Miss.'

Something was troubling Vita's thoughts. It took a moment to remember, but then the feeling of panic rose sharply.

'I must go to the nursery, Swain. There may be a dangerous medicine there. Please. It's urgent. It must be kept from the children. We must hurry.'

'Come,' said Swain. He took Vita's arm and propelled her through the complicated geography of Pemberton at a speed that left Vita with only the blurry impression of staircases, passageways and grand paintings flashing by. They burst into the nursery kitchen and found Netty, still looking tearful, making toast. Mary-Ann and William were sitting at the table.

'Netty, is there any medicine here for the children?' Vita gasped.

Netty, standing with a toasting fork over the fire, could only gaze helplessly at them. Mary-Ann and William looked on astonished.

'Only the night time medicine, Miss,' Netty finally said. 'Master William has it with his cocoa if he can't sleep.'

'And you haven't given any to him yet? Or to his sister?'

'No, Miss, I couldn't find it. Mr Billings brings it in a blue bottle. It's always kept up there,' she pointed to a high cupboard.

Swain strode over and opened the cupboard door, but the shelf inside was empty.

Vita spoke gently to the girl, who was close to tears. 'Netty, do you know what could have happened to the medicine?'

Netty now gave in to helpless weeping, lifting the hem of her apron to dab her face. 'Miss Hartley came' she blurted between shuddering sobs, 'Miss Hartley came and took it to her room.'

*W*hen, much later, Vita finally remembered the note and knocked on the Chef's door, it opened to reveal Dr Zecker as well as Monsieur Picard. The chef's pantry was a small windowless storage space crammed with packages, boxes and jars. There was barely room for a single chair, but three had been installed.

'I have asked you both here to prove my innocence!' the chef declared. 'I beg you to stay. I have devised a proof that there was absolutely no contamination of the seafood last night. None whatsoever!'

'What is he going to do?' Zecker asked, in German. 'He is overwrought, I fear.'

'You think I am too dramatic, non? But I wish to persuade you that my seafood - the good seafood of France is healthy and good. It harmed nobody last night.'

'Ask him to calm himself, please,' Dr Zecker told Vita, 'I dread some moment of madness to follow.'

'Here is my proposal,' said the chef. He lifted a domed cover to reveal a plate of oysters and assorted seafood. 'I propose that I should eat this food taken directly from the dining table last night. I shall eat it before you to prove that I am unharmed and my health perfectly undamaged.'

'The man is mad, I think,' Zecker said. 'This proves nothing. This proposal is most unscientific.'

'See!' cried the chef, 'I eat it! It is delicious and good in all ways!' He swallowed two oysters in a row, cracked the head from a prawn and tore the flesh out of its body with his teeth, chewing with exaggerated relish. 'I could eat all this and several buckets more, and still I would be in the very best of health. I swear this is the truth!'

'What a performance,' Zecker said. 'I hope he does not expect me to sit here in this cupboard and watch him consume buckets full of shellfish. If it does not make him ill, the sight will certainly damage my own health!'

'Eat some yourself! It will not harm you. I would give this to an invalid with absolute confidence,' the chef declared, continuing to crack shells and swallow crustaceans. He waved a plate of oysters under their noses.

'I do not eat the flesh of living creatures,' Zecker remarked, 'it is a matter of principle.'

The chef paused in his chewing. 'Not even oysters?' he asked, when Vita translated.

'No living thing,' the doctor confirmed.

'No meat? No fish? He has no life at all!' declared Monsieur Picard, and he continued eating shellfish from the plate.

'There were other dishes eaten last night,' Vita said. 'Before the seafood there was a soup, I recall.'

'A choice of two to be precise: mock turtle and consommé de volailles,' said the chef. 'I have some of both here. Do you wish me to take some soup also?'

'This is ridiculous!' Zecker declared.

'It would confuse the outcome if you now consumed two

soups as well. There would be no way of knowing which, if any of them, caused you to be ill. If you did become ill,' Vita pointed out.

The chef could see she was right.

'Perhaps the doctor would try the soups?' he challenged.

'Certainly not. Both are made from living things,' Zecker said, once the idea was translated.

'I shall take the soup, then,' Vita said.

'I do not allow this,' Zecker objected. 'What would your aunt say to this?'

'It will be a useful part of the experiment, surely?' And without waiting, Vita seized the first small cup of soup and swallowed it. She was about to take the second when Zecker reached across, took the cup and tossed back the soup with his eyes closed and a look of disgust.

'Why did you drink it?' Vita asked.

'Mock turtle. What is it? What is a mock turtle? I know it is a living creature and therefore against my principles, but I should like to know what sort of a creature it is exactly. Especially if it is to make me ill.' Zecker declared.

But the mock turtle soup did not make Dr Zecker ill. It was Vita who, only a few minutes later, had to run from the room.

CHAPTER 45

'*I*t is a mild case, and you have a sound constitution, there is nothing to worry about,' Zecker was saying an hour later.

Vita had been put to bed in the Yellow Room. Her Aunt had been told she was ill, as had their hosts. Dr Zecker had, however, not explained the real cause of her sudden illness.

'You would not be saying that if I were Miss Von Diepentahl!' she muttered. 'Lotti would have a dozen footmen running about and everyone would be wringing their hands outside the door.'

The doctor smiled. 'The strength of your irritation is a very good sign.'

'We have proved beyond doubt that the consommé was what caused this sickness,' the chef declared, when, shortly after, he was admitted to the room. 'I myself am in perfect health as you can see. The shellfish - I consumed a large quantity - was delicious. I have no ill effects whatsoever.'

'Good for you,' Vita said, 'but could you stop talking about the soup, please? It still came from your kitchen, Monsieur Picard.'

176

'But the doctor has found that the soup – but only the consommé, Dr Zecker showed no ill effects from the *mock turtle* soup – was poisoned by a malicious hand! Someone added a poison to it!' Monsieur Picard declared, waving his arms as if triumphantly conducting an orchestra.

'What? How can you tell that? Who would do such a thing?' Vita asked.

'While you were...*indisposed*,' Zecker said, 'I searched, with the help of Herr Swain, through all the empty medicine bottles found in the cellar. Most had contained Laudanum, but one bottle was brown and not blue. Its label was in German and had contained a very powerful purging medicine. Something specifically formulated to produce the effect you so unfortunately experienced, Miss Carew. I believe it is this that caused the dramatic reaction of so many diners to the soup.'

'Not the soup itself,' cried the chef, 'the soup itself was good. It was excellent!'

'Could we stop talking about the soup now please?' Vita said, weakly.

'My kitchen is not to blame!' said the chef. 'It is not to be held responsible. Someone maliciously poisoned my food, but before it was poisoned, it was wholesome and delicious. And now I leave you, brave Miss Carew, to recover, but as you do so, please remember that I shall always be grateful. Always!'

Monsieur bowed and marched out of the room.

'Alas, things may not be as simple as he thinks,' Dr Zecker remarked.

'What do you mean?' asked his patient, lying back on her pillows.

'I have a feeling that the chef may not escape punishment, fairly or not.'

'But why? You have proved he did nothing wrong.'

Dr Zecker shook his head. 'It is easier to blame a chef for bad oysters than it is to explain how an emetic found its way into the soup at a grand dinner party. I believe I know who put it there, incidentally.'

The German doctor frowned and looked at his shoes. 'Of course one cannot be *entirely* certain,' he added.

'Who?'

'I believe it to have been Miss Von Diepentahl,' the doctor said. 'She did not aim to kill anyone, only to...to disrupt the evening.'

Vita could only blink at him. 'She certainly achieved that!'

Zecker only raised an eyebrow.

'But the effect was serious on Miss Von Diepentahl herself. She was badly poisoned!'

Again the doctor did not reply.

'Hers was a serious case of poisoning, was it not?'

Zecker still said nothing. He looked away, appearing to take an interest in something on the mantelpiece.

'Dr Zecker?'

The doctor looked back with an inscrutable expression. 'She is a great artist,' he said, 'and an actress of enormous skill. That is all I will say.'

'But why? Why would she do such a thing?'

'That I cannot answer.'

Vita lay for a moment looking up at the faded cherubs on the fourposter bed. 'I think I might know. I heard her talking to the Italian gentleman.'

'Signor Ricci?'

'Yes. It was immediately after the engagement was announced. He told her his great sopranos were always unmarried. The public did not care for a soprano who was married, or even engaged to be married, he said. Would that be enough to make her take such extreme action?'

'Quite enough. The Von Diepentahls have spoken of little else but Signor Ricci for months. He is a god in their world. Their main purpose in coming to England was to cultivate his acquaintance and they were all triumphant when he accepted the invitation to come here to Pemberton Hall. Fraulein Karlotta would have been horrified to learn that he would only work with an artiste who was unmarried. Her aunts also.'

'You believe that Lotti was willing to poison her fellow guests *and herself* in order to break off her engagement? It sounds absurd.'

'You are correct, Miss Carew. It does sound unbelievable,' Zecker said.

'Who will you tell?'

'Nobody. What is to be gained? My theory cannot be proved. If accused, Miss Diepentahl would deny everything.'

Vita gaped at the doctor, who busied himself pouring her a glass of water. 'If you tell no-one, Lotti will escape unpunished, and the chef will take all the blame.'

'I'm afraid he will be blamed whatever I do. The chef must be sacrificed in order to preserve the household's reputation. Sadly, such things are not so unusual in a grand household.'

A silence fell as both contemplated this injustice.

Vita sat up in bed. 'Why do you choose to work for Miss Von Diepentahl and her aunts, Dr Zecker? Surely there is more rewarding work to be found than following grand ladies from town to town?'

Zecker now occupied himself with repacking his medical bag. 'Perhaps there is. And I may seek it. I have encouraged you to pursue your interest in science, Miss Carew, or at least I hope I have, but you need also to know that science, and medicine in particular, is not – as we say in German – is not always a rose garden. I have had difficulties. I worked in a hospital and there contracted a bad infection. Later in private practice I lost a patient ... let me only say that I lost a patient I should have been able to save, and one I cared deeply for. I had not the heart to practice for a while. Miss Von Diepentahl and her aunts offered me a return to medicine and for that I am grateful to them. But now, well you imply there is more important work to be done, and you are quite correct. I shall not stay with them much longer.'

'They will be sad to lose you, Dr Zecker.'

The doctor snapped his bag shut with a reverberating click. 'Only until they find another 'ridiculous tame doctor'. That is what Dr Mills called me, and he was not entirely wrong, I admit it.'

Vita looked at him in surprise.

He shrugged. 'I understand English better than people think,' he said. 'Now you should rest and drink only water until your appetite returns. And one more thing. Never do that again. Never swallow something to test if it is poisoned! Do you understand me? It is not scientific and next time you may kill yourself.'

'I promise, Doctor.'

*A*fter Zecker had left, Aunt Louisa and Lady Felicity visited to say goodnight.

'Oh dear, this is a chilly room!' Felicity exclaimed with a shudder. 'My apologies, Vita. Now that the other guests are gone you would be most welcome to move.'

'I have become fond of the Yellow Room,' Vita said. 'Even the cherubs seem friendly now.'

Lady Felicity looked doubtful. 'It used to be called the Emperor's bed. It came from France. Napoleon is supposed to have slept in it – not here, of course – though personally I was never convinced. I believe it was one of Dickie's grand-father's purchases.'

'And are you recovered, Dear?' asked her Aunt.

'Yes, I am only a little bruised and tired. It was very shocking, what happened to Billings. I saw Dr Mills return.'

'He has done everything necessary. Billings died immedi-ately, Mills said. Nobody would have wished for him to meet such an end, but he almost killed Dickie, and that evil medi-cine would have killed the children…And then, of course, there is Miss Hartley,' Louisa took her friend's arm to comfort her.

'How is Lord Pemberton?' asked Vita.

'He is much more himself. Mills says there may be lasting effects. He has been dosed with high quantities of this medicine for a long period. It may be difficult to stop.' Lady Pemberton seemed to lose the thread of her thoughts for a moment, but then she smiled at Vita and patted her hand. 'The police will have to come, but not until tomorrow. Now, you need to rest and I for one can take no more tonight. We shall leave you to sleep. You have been very brave, Vita. Tomorrow is soon enough to discuss these events further. Mills says Dickie should rest until the afternoon, but if you would be so good as to stay until tea time, he would like then to speak to everyone together.'

THE MAIDS who opened the curtains and brought tea the next morning also carried with them a blouse and skirt to replace Vita's now battle-torn day dress.

'The mistress wanted you to have these Miss,' the older one said. 'We mended the rip in the sleeve of your white dress, but the lovely new evening gown will need a proper cleaning.'

Vita had not given much thought to her clothes. 'How kind,' she said.

'You did us a favour, Miss. Nobody wanted him to lose his life, but between you and me we're all glad to see Billings gone. Nasty piece of work, he was. And free with his hands. None of us liked him. Breakfast is in the big dining room, today.'

In the dining room Vita found the cheerful bustle of a

generous breakfast well under way. The children were there as well as Lord and Lady Pemberton, who even sat together. From the first moment of her arrival Vita was surprised to find that she attracted the enthusiastic attention of every waiting footman. Swain himself walked her to her place at the table and selected her food from the chafing dishes, an honour usually accorded only to the head of the household or possibly visiting royalty. Queen Victoria in her portrait certainly noticed, but even she seemed less critical today. Aunt Louisa caught Vita's eye across the table and winked. The atmosphere at Pemberton Hall could hardly have been more different.

CHAPTER 47

'We have the day to ourselves, it seems,' her aunt told her at the table. 'I shall continue the portrait – whatever the circumstances I hate to leave a piece unfinished. It is a personal rule. Besides I would like to be on hand for Felicity. And you, Vita, how will you pass the day?'

'I shall seek out the paintings on your list,' Vita said.

Dr Zecker looked up from his fruit salad. 'I have asked Her Ladyship's permission to examine the architecture of the Hall. Perhaps we could combine our activities,' he suggested.

'Good idea,' Aunt Louisa agreed, 'but take William and Mary-Ann with you. They need distraction. They cannot ride today and they will be at loose ends.'

Mary-Ann, as it turned out, had an invitation from her cousin, but William agreed with enthusiasm to accompany the German doctor and Vita. They set out first for the folly, a picturesque ruin on the only slope that overlooked the house. It had been built to offer the ideal view of the Hall, whose great width showed its most impressive expanse from this angle.

'It is a fine prospect,' Dr Zecker remarked, 'though

perhaps better enjoyed when the wind is less biting. I am not sure my ears will still be in place if the wind blasts them for much longer.'

'I wish I could speak German,' William remarked, 'I only know one word.'

'And what is your one word?' Dr Zecker asked in English.

'*Himmel*,' William said. 'It means heaven.'

'That is certainly a good word,' Zecker said. 'Would you like another?'

William was occupying himself by running up the folly's ruined stairs and jumping off. He leapt from the fifth step and landed in the muddy grass before saying. 'Yes, please.'

'*Springen*,' said the doctor, 'that means jump!'

'*Springen*!' William said, pleased with the new addition, '*springen*!' and he climbed up and hurled himself down again.

Driven back towards the house by the cold, they noticed a cart driving away from the house. It had trunks on it. They were too far away to see the passenger, but William seemed to know something.

'We will have plain food today,' he remarked. 'Mama says a new chef will be coming but until then Cook will make our food. Her food is very good but it is not French. She makes steak and kidney pudding. I like that very much. If I ask her, she makes roly-poly pudding with custard.'

'What is this roly-poly pudding?' Zecker asked him.

'Sponge and jam – it is delicious! You would like it. Everyone likes it,' William told him.

Vita watched the cart until it was hidden by the trees on the drive. *I did nothing to help the chef*, she thought with a pang.

'You should not blame yourself for this,' Zecker said,

reading her thoughts and speaking aside. 'Come! We must hide from this terrible wind and find some of those paintings indoors.'

William knew the paintings well, though his art appreciation was brisk, to put it mildly. He led them straight to 'The Shepherdess', which was number three on Vita's list. It was a large canvas over a fireplace in one of the reception rooms.

'She doesn't look like a real shepherdess, does she?' William remarked as the three of them stood in a row and studied it.

It was true. The young woman in the painting was dressed for a fashionable party, not herding sheep.

'She does not look strong, either,' the doctor said, 'her waist is very small, and she is pale.'

'Why did they paint her, then?' William asked.

'Shepherdesses represented innocent simplicity and the lovely countryside, I believe,' Zecker told him. Vita translated. William looked unconvinced.

'But what of the quality of the painting itself?' Vita asked. All three stepped forward and peered more closely at the brushwork.

'I think it's too brown,' William said.

'I agree,' said the doctor. For some reason this made all of them laugh.

'My favourite painting is 'Eternal Star', I'll show you that one. It's much better than this,' William ran off, along a corridor and into a small sitting room. 'Eternal Star' turned out to be an Arab stallion, painted almost life-size. The canvas dominated the room. The beautiful horse, flaring its nostrils and looking as if it might bolt at any moment, was held by a calm groom. The man looked out at the viewer, with an expression of quiet pride. The horse was rolling its eye, and seemed full of dangerously pent-up energy.

'It is magnificent, but the horse is better painted than the man, I think,' Zecker said.

'Yes. That's why I like it,' William agreed.

Luncheon, delicious but in the English and not the French style, as William had predicted, interrupted their studies of Art History and afterwards Dr Zecker led William and Vita on a brisk tour of the Hall's outstanding architectural features. The shape and positioning of the windows, the plaster mouldings of fruit and flowers, the panelling, the turret, the pillared entrance with its stone steps were all visited and their architectural derivations explained. It was a cheerful afternoon. William listened with surprising curiosity as Vita translated, only pausing every now and then to jump off something or run in a circle.

They were summoned to the library just as his interest began to wane.

'I must take my leave,' Zecker said, as they walked towards the entrance hall, 'my train leaves at four.'

'You will not come to hear Lord Pemberton speak to everyone?'

'No. I am aware of what is likely to be said. I have an appointment this evening in London. I must say goodbye. And thank you for a pleasant day, after a rather too dramatic visit.'

'Thank you for your encouragement, Dr Zecker.'

They shook hands, the doctor bowing as he did so. 'I feel that we shall meet again. So until then,' he said and turned away.

CHAPTER 48

'*M*uch as we all wish to put recent distressing events behind us,' Lord Pemberton began, 'one or two matters do need to be clarified.'

Swain, Cook and Mrs Parks, together with all the maids, kitchen staff and footmen, stood to attention on one side of the room, while family and guests sat on sofas around the fireplace.

'To begin with Billings,' his Lordship went on. 'It seems he was conniving with a pharmacist and overbuying the medicines I was prescribed. The excess he sold at a profit, some of it to the unfortunate governess, Miss…'

' …*Hartley*…' his wife quietly prompted him.

'Yes, Miss Hartley. Mills thinks the pharmacist sold Billings an excessively strong solution of the medicine in error. Billings either did not notice, or did not understand – his reading was weak. The exact extent of his involvement in the death of the unfortunate Miss Hartley is unclear. I suspect that he recklessly supplied her with the same dangerously concentrated medicine he administered to me and which, but for the quick-wittedness of Miss Carew, might have poisoned my children as well. I blame myself for a great deal of this, incidentally.'

Lady Felicity put her hand on her husband's shoulder.

'Billings was a loyal servant in my army days. I employed him to help with my care. His regime was effective up to a point. He appeared to have my best interests at heart. He had, however, been dosing me with strong medicine for some months. Dr Mills now thinks the dose was steadily increased. Perhaps Billings felt I might dispense with his services if I recovered. Whatever his thinking, he exerted increasing power. It took the crisis of last night to make this clear.'

His Lordship paused, as if still considering all that had happened. 'His fall was a dreadful accident. I shall arrange a funeral here in the chapel. He was a good man who lost his way. I have spoken already to the police. The Inspector will interview those of you who witnessed the accident, shortly. He will be asking questions about Miss Hartley as well, of course.'

The housekeeper, Mrs Parks, seemed to sway a little on her feet. Swain brought her a chair, but she waved it away and left the room.

'I turn now to the sickness at dinner,' his Lordship continued. 'Many guests were afflicted, Miss Von Diepentahl – our guest of honour – in particular. I doubt we shall ever have a complete explanation. Suspicion fell on the seafood – it generally does. Whatever one's opinion, it must be acknowledged that distinguished guests suffered as a result of the food served at Pemberton Hall's table. It is a public disgrace, and will be difficult to overcome.'

Vita tried to interrupt, but his Lordship continued.

'Whatever the explanation, Pemberton Hall's reputation – and that of my family – will inevitably suffer. We shall weather the scandal surrounding the events of the past few days as best we can, but there are certain steps that must be taken. Since the ultimate responsibility for all that is eaten at Pemberton's table falls to him, I shall, with regret, be replacing Monsieur Picard.'

Before Vita could object again, Dickie Pemberton held up his hand.

He turned to Vita. 'Miss Carew, my family is so far in your debt that I hardly know where to begin. Dr Zecker told me that your assistance in treating my collapse was invaluable. If there is anything we can do to repay you...'

Vita, eager to defend the chef, began to speak, but was cut short by her aunt who replied, 'Dickie, Felicity, if I might have a word in private?'

'Of course,' his Lordship said, 'but before that I have a small gift for Miss Carew.'

Felicity handed her husband a small package. He passed it with some ceremony to William, who ran across the room to deliver it.

'I know what it is! Open it, Miss Carew!'

It was a new pair of spectacles. A notably more robust and stylish pair than she had lost the day before.

'But however did you find a new pair so quickly?' she asked, amazed.

'All the credit for that,' said his Lordship, 'must go to Swain.'

The butler nodded in modest acknowledgment. 'They may not be perfect,' he told her. 'An oculist friend worked all morning and used your broken lenses to estimate what you would need.'

'Another upshot of these events concerns my son, Alexander,' Lord Pemberton continued, looking serious again. 'You will see that he is not among us. He has followed Miss Von Diepentahl and her aunts to London. Miss Von

Diepentahl has written formally ending the betrothal. It has been a great blow to our son. He has little hope of saving their engagement, but nothing would stop him trying.'

At this point Lord Pemberton began to cough. He already looked tired and frail. Now he bent forward in his wheeled chair and gasped for air.

'That is enough for now, I think,' Lady Pemberton told the room.

The family filed out with Swain pushing his master's chair, and were followed by the staff. Vita and her aunt were left alone.

'Aunt, please try to convince them that Monsieur Picard is not to blame.'

'How can you be certain of that? The soup affected you too, when you tried it.'

'Yes, but Dr Zecker and Monsieur Picard both believe it had been adulterated – someone added an emetic to it.'

'Vita! Who in the world would do such a thing as that?'

Vita attempted to explain, but somehow in daylight Dr Zecker's theory that Lotti had slipped an emetic into the consommé sounded absurd.

'Good Lord, I never heard such nonsense!' her aunt remarked. 'I told you that German doctor was a strange little person. What an imagination! I'm not convinced that Miss Diepentahl did any such thing. I am, on the other hand, perfectly willing to believe that she ended the betrothal because it might endanger her prospects as a singer. And just between us, Vita, I am not sorry. There was something in that young woman's face that simply would not allow it to sit alongside Alexander's on the page. Try as I might, I couldn't make the double portrait work. It seemed an ill omen.'

CHAPTER 49

The breakfast room at Eden Street, though many times smaller than the grand dining room at Pemberton Hall, was every bit as pleasant a place to eat toast and marmalade, as Aunt Louisa remarked a few days later.

Vita slid *Studies in Fossil Botany* under the table and agreed.

'We have a busy day, Vita. I must ask you to run an errand immediately after breakfast, and at 10 o'clock we catch the London train.'

'Do we?'

'Yes. To visit Miss Von Diepentahl and her aunts. They have asked to see the portrait.'

'The *engagement* portrait?'

'Yes. Miss Von Diepentahl is interested in acquiring it.'

'How do you know?'

'I offered it to her myself. Why not? Individually, the portraits are rather fine work, though I say it myself. It is only that the two faces do not work together.'

'And the errand?'

Her Aunt handed Vita a bunch of keys. 'Take these keys to the address on the label and give them to Monsieur Picard.'

'Monsieur Picard the chef?'

'Yes. He is now in my employ.'

'But how? How did that happen?'

Her aunt occupied herself with toast and butter. 'Felicity and I came to an arrangement. They have housed him nearby and provided him with a generous allowance. He has agreed to cook for us. It took a little negotiating, but they were very fair in the end. Oh, and they have also set up an account for you at the University bookshop – twenty pounds – for text-books. But you must resist rushing there immediately – there is a train to catch!'

In London, the Von Diepentahls stayed near Regent's Park in the elegant townhouse of a German friend. The staff seemed to be German too. They were greeted in accented English by a footman and led into a marble floored entrance hall with a curving staircase. Every surface seemed to be festooned with huge floral arrangements. They covered the tables and windowsills and stood in pots on the floors as well, filling the atmosphere with the florist's smell of roses and fresh green-ery. They were shown to an opulent room with windows overlooking the park. This, too, had vases of hothouse flowers on every surface.

As was her usual habit, Louisa immediately began inspecting the paintings. Most were portraits of unsmiling gentlemen surrounded by symbols of knowledge and good works, in the familiar way, but there were two much older scenes of rural life that caught her attention. It was fully twenty minutes before Miss Von Diepentahl appeared. They knew she was approaching because a little dog she addressed as *Fritzi*, ran barking energetically into the room before her. He ran to Louisa and Vita in greeting before finding an interesting object under the piano and taking it secretively into a corner to chew.

'Ah, you are here! I wish you welcome Miss Brocklehurst and Miss Carew. I am happy indeed to see you both. Shall we drink some coffee? Or would you prefer tea?'

Both were ordered of the footman, who left followed by the dog.

Karlotta settled herself on a sofa by the fireplace and they sat opposite. An ormulu clock ticked on the mantelpiece underlining the pauses in the conversation. At first, it was hard going.

'And how is your health now?' Louisa enquired. 'You are completely recovered? It is more than a week now since ...'

Karlotta seemed to flinch briefly at the memory. She looked out of the window. Soft winter sunshine was bathing the park and the carriages passing on the road outside. The clock ticked. 'Several days I was confined to my bed, but I am feeling much better now, thank you. Yesterday I was in the park and the evening before I went to the opera. My strength is returning, but it has been slow.'

The clock chimed a musical quarter hour. A German tune, Vita thought, not having heard it before. Distantly in the house, another clock echoed and a little later one even further away sang out a wooden cuckoo call. Vita was trying not to catch her aunt's eye.

'And how is everyone at Pemberton Hall?' Lotti asked.

The wording of the question was so studiedly neutral that Louisa hardly knew how to answer.

Vita was glad of the distraction when Fritzi bounded back into the room and went to search of his toy in the far corner.

'Sir Richard has been unwell, but is recovering now. Everyone else is in good health.'

'But there was a most unfortunate death, yes?'

Vita and her aunt hesistated, wondering how much Lotti had heard.

'The governess, yes,' Louisa confirmed, eventually.

'And do they know...?'

'It seems she took too much of a sleeping medicine.'

Lotti looked at them sharply. 'Ah, so it was nothing to do with the dinner?'

'The doctors say not.'

'And everyone else in the family is in good health?' Lotti asked this question looking down at the lace edging on her sleeve. She straightened its delicate filigree loops, stroking them flat along her wrist.

'All well, yes. The family send their best wishes for your continued recovery.'

Lotti nodded, but did not look up. The clock ticked and Fritzi could be heard chewing with concentration on whatever he had found. Carriage wheels rumbled outside.

The footman returned with a maid who set silver tea and coffee pots and tiny cups and saucers on a sideboard, poured the drinks, and carried cups to the ladies. There was no conversation during this activity. Fritzi detected biscuits on the tray and ran over to sit as close to them as possible.

The ladies sipped. The maid and footman left the room.

CHAPTER 50

'*I* have brought the portrait I was making,' Aunt Louisa told Karlotta. She watched how this was received. Karlotta looked interested. 'It is incomplete, obviously, but I wondered whether ...'

'... I should love to see it!'

'I wondered whether it might have associations that were too ... unfortunate' said Louisa, 'too upsetting.'

'Certainly it was an unhappy visit,' Karlotta said, but her eyes were shining now and she looked eagerly at the portfolio Louisa was holding.

'I should not like to risk stirring unhappy memories...'

'No indeed. I should like to see it, nonetheless.'

'It might be difficult for you to see ... the other person in the portrait.'

Lotti was leaning forward now, almost reaching out for the portfolio. She controlled her eagerness a little at this and said solemnly, 'I believe I am sufficiently strong to bear it, Frau Brocklehurst. May I see?'

Louisa did not, however, hand the portfolio to Lotti.

Instead she undid its ribbons herself and opening it, displayed the portrait upright against its black bindings.

'Oh!' Lotti jumped a little in surprise, her hand at her throat. She leaned forward, taking in all the portrait's details. She looked, Vita noticed, only at the image of her own face, inclining towards it, her eyes scarcely skimming over Alexander's image on the other side. Louisa said nothing. As an experienced portrait artist she knew when to intervene on such an occasions, and when to remain silent. After several minutes Lotti sighed. She sat back and smiled at Louisa in undisguised delight. 'But it is wonderful! Wonderful! It is not like other portraits I have had made. In those I am a wooden thing, a doll, but here I am so alive! So ... oh, I don't know the word for it ... so *bright*. The light seems to shine through me. I am delighted with this, Miss Brocklehurst. It is truly marvellous. I cannot wait to show my aunts - they will be enchanted, utterly enchanted.'

'Do I take it that you would like to keep this portrait, Miss Von Diepentahl?'

'Keep it! But yes, decidedly I must keep it. It is marvellous.'

'There is the slight issue of ...' Here Louisa inclined her head very slightly towards Alexander's face, on the other side of the picture.

A little frown swept Lotti's brow. 'Yes,' she said, 'sadly, this part is not acceptable to me any longer.'

Louisa began to close the portfolio.

'Oh, but why do you close it?'

'If it is not acceptable ...'

'But only that part. The rest is admirable. It pleases me very much indeed!'

'But the painting consists of both faces. The composition is a balanced one, they both form one image.'

Lotti looked pained. Her hands flopped irritably into her lap. Then an idea seemed to enter her mind. 'Would it not be possible to ...'

'... to?'

'... to *amend* the painting in any way?'

'I don't think so,' Louisa said, sounding as if this were an unheard of suggestion.

'Excuse me for asking this of an artist, Miss Brocklehurst, but could you not ... find a way to separate the faces? One could perhaps simply be removed, yes? Or another image could be painted over ... perhaps my little Fritzi!'

'It is a watercolour. A watercolour would be ruined by overpainting,' Louisa told her.

'Or cut? Perhaps it could just be cut.'

'I could not allow it. I'm afraid it would destroy the integrity of the work.'

'Oh dear!'

The clock chimed a tinkling half hour tune, and off in the distance another boomed its own chorus, followed by the ever-energetic cuckoo. *How does anyone bear it?* Vita wondered, but she said, 'Is there no way of preserving this delightful portrait Aunt? Lotti is right to admire it, and it seems a great shame that it now seems likely to be destroyed.'

'Destroyed! But no!' Lotti cried. 'Please do reconsider, Frau Brocklehurst.'

Aunt Louisa closed the portfolio and tied its ribbons. She set it on the sofa beside her and brushed the creases from her skirt, considering. 'It would be a shame to do so. I admit I am quite pleased with it myself. But I cannot allow my work to be compromised, you, as an artist yourself, would understand this.'

'Of course!' Karlotta said.

Fritzi suddenly uttered a series of loud, sharp barks and ran to the door, which was thrown open to reveal the German aunts.

'There you are darling girl!' cried Gabrielle. 'We are so late! The carriage was unable to move for the crowds all along the park. We thought we would never get back. We thought we would miss our little Vita's visit with her talented aunt. I'm so glad we have finally arrived.'

After a flurry of greetings, the aunts settled into the sofas and begged to see the portrait for themselves. When it was presented, they were just as enthusiastic, though they attempted to mute their comments slightly in deference to Lotti's feelings at seeing the face of her no-longer-beloved beside her own.

'There is no question at all of it being destroyed. That cannot be allowed to happen, surely,' Gabriella told Vita. She translated, but Louisa was looking stern, and did not reply.

The aunts and Lotti spoke between themselves in German for some minutes. Vita sipping her coffee and listening only discreetly.

'I have a suggestion for Miss Brocklehurst,' Tante Gabriella eventually said, 'translate, please, Vita. Ask her whether she would consider allowing the portrait to be divided, by ... *trimming*. In this manner we believe the lovely image of Lotti could successfully be preserved and displayed as it should be. Naturally, we would make recognition of your aunt's generosity in allowing this.'

Louisa, when this was explained, seemed not to be willing.

The German ladies spoke together for a few more moments. 'We would double the fee,' Tante Gabrielle said, 'tell your aunt we will pay twice if she will ... rearrange the portrait in this manner.'

Aunt Louisa listened unflinching while this was translated. She sighed, and turned the portfolio around so that she could study the portrait herself. The other ladies held their breath.

On consideration she agreed that she *might* be able to re-trim the portrait, though it pained her to do so. She would take it away and see what could be done.

At this point a footman entered quietly and coughed in the well-practised way of a man delivering a subtle, but important message.

'Ah! My singing master is here. It is time for my voice exercises. I have a concert next week. I hope you will excuse me if I entrust you to my aunts and bid you goodbye.'

'Of course,' Aunt Louisa said.

Lotti began to leave, but seemed to feel the note being struck by her departure was not quite as she wished. Turning, she said, 'It has been a pleasure to make your acquaintance of course, even though the ... circumstances ...' Here she broke off, but then continued with a little sob in her voice, '... even though our visit did not end *quite* as expected.'

With that she left the room, her skirts billowing behind her and her little dog running at her heels. It was not quite an operatic exit, but it was satisfactorily dramatic.

CHAPTER 51

*Q*uiet returned to the parlour for a moment. The ticking of the clock reasserted itself.

'There can be no doubt at all that the portrait is very fine, Frau Brocklehurst, very fine indeed. We are most grateful to you,' Tante Gabrielle said. Before Vita could translate she continued, 'But it has been a very trying time for us, this visit to Pemberton Hall, you will understand this.'

'Of course,' said Aunt Louisa, when she heard. 'It has been regrettable in many ways.'

Tante Gabrielle looked piercingly at Louisa, but said nothing more except, 'I shall be needed to sit with Lotti in the music room, so I will bid you goodbye. I hope we meet under better circumstances next time. And goodbye to our faithful little translator, too, you have served us well, Vita. Remember what I said, take off your eyeglasses a little more and do not read so much. Try to be a little more light-hearted. Then you may be quite attractive.'

To their surprise Tante Adelina did not leave the room with her sister. Instead she went to the piano and began to play a little flowing piece. But she broke off after only a few bars and returned, sitting where Lotti had been before.

'Vita, I would like you to tell your aunt that I am going to speak to you both in confidence now. Will you tell her this? Will you ask her not to speak too freely of what I say? I am not asking her to keep all to herself, only to treat what I say with some delicacy.'

They agreed. Little Tante Adelina took a deep breath and held her hands in her lap. She pressed her lips together as if summoning determination before she spoke. 'Lotti has not had a good upbringing. There, I have said it. She has been brought up in an isolated household with no children her own age to play with, surrounded by adults who adore her and have never crossed her in any way. To sum it up, she has been spoilt. Her talents have, if anything, worsened the situation. She has been swept from music conservatory to concert hall for many years, with nothing about her but adoration and encouragement and the result is a young woman who is given to whims and light-headedness and who, I'm afraid little understands the feelings of people around her.'

'But she did genuinely have feelings for Alexander, surely,' Louisa said.

Tante Adelina nodded, 'Certainly, but she had not considered the consequences of what she was doing. It was – I'm afraid most things are for Karlotta – a lovely game. She would become engaged to this handsome and talented young man. There would be parties! She had not considered it any further than that, I imagine. She is not malicious, you understand, she simply has no ... no bearings on life. She is not nearly as mature as you are, Vita, for example.'

All this was translated, leaving Louisa and Vita taken aback by the little German lady's forthright explanation.

'And her illness?' Vita dared to ask.

Adelina shrugged. 'It may have been genuine to begin with, but later - who knows?'

'Surely she would not playact something so very serious.'

'Well, as I said, consequences are not something Karlotta dwells on. Now, I shall say no more, except that I also think the portrait is a very impressive work of art, and I personally shall see to it that the terms of purchase briefly discussed this morning are adhered to. Now, goodbye to you both. And Vita, if I may add my own advice,' Adelina took Vita's hand in both her own, 'you must wear your eyeglasses whenever you need them, and read as much as you like. I wish you both well.'

In the carriage on the way to the station, Vita could see her aunt smiling. Even though the interior was dim and Louisa was wearing a large hat, her eyes were shining beneath its brim.

'Are you satisfied, Aunt, with the arrangement?'

'Yes, I believe I am,' her aunt said, mildly enough, though her expression was not so mild. She looked, in fact, extremely pleased. 'I shall separate the erstwhile sweethearts' faces and frame them separately. Both likenesses will look far better apart. They never worked together as a composition.'

'You have no qualms about compromising the painting's integrity, then?'

'None, since they paid me double!'

'Aunt!'

'Felicity has already offered a generous fee for Alexander's portrait. All in all, I shall be very generously compensated for this little watercolour. I never took to it, myself. I shall be perfectly happy to cut it up and sincerely hope never to see it again. I only regret that my poor Godson had to have his heart broken as part of the transaction.'

'Did Lady Pemberton say how Alexander was?'

'He rides a lot, she says, and plays the piano for hours every day.'

'Poor Alexander. He truly loved Karlotta, I suppose.'

'Yes. He is a serious young man. He will need time to recover his spirits completely, though I am told there is a lovely young violinist who occasionally assists him with his compositions.'

At King's Cross station, a pale sun pushed slanted beams through the glass arches of the roof.

'Come, Vita' said her aunt, leading the way towards their platform. 'My studio is calling me from Eden Street and you must have reading to do. With a bit of luck Monsieur Picard has installed himself in the kitchen and prepared something rather good for dinner.'

She was right. The house was filled with the smell of roast chicken as they entered. Bread had been baked, and in the background there was a hint of something sweeter. It later proved to be the lightest and most delicious hazelnut meringue.

AFTERWORD

I based Pemberton Hall on Wimpole Hall, a stately home owned by the National Trust near Cambridge, where I live in the UK. The paintings in the story are real paintings I saw there.

You can see images I collected while I was doing the research for Poison at Pemberton Hall on my website fransmithwriting.co.uk.

One of the joys of crime writing is that it sends the mind whirring off in wicked directions. What fun to wander Wimpole picking sites for poisonings and fights and wondering how much Laudanum would induce a coma.

I hope you enjoyed reading the results.

Best wishes,

Fran Smith

ACKNOWLEDGMENTS

As usual I must thank my early readers for their time and careful feedback, my proofreaders for their attention to detail and my writing partner Tricia McBride for the regular nudges I need to keep me going.

And Chris, who does all the domestic stuff I ignore when I'm writing and doesn't mind talking plot details at 5 am.

REVIEWS

Independent authors need reviews. Reader reviews are the best way to spread the news about our books.

So, if you enjoyed Poison at Pemberton Hall, a review or rating is always very welcome. It's quick and easy to leave one, and it means a lot.

Thank you in advance, Dear Reader.

Fran